ADVANCE PRAISE FOR

The Soviet Circus Comes to Havana and Other Stories

IN *The Soviet Circus Comes to Havana,* Virgil Suarez paints a vivid picture of the beauty and terror of revolutionary Cuba and exile from that 'solitary island floating away into a blue expanse.' These elegantly crafted coming-of-age stories richly illustrate that the first losses of life are among the hardest to bear.

RITA CIRESI, author of *Pink Slip* and *Sometimes I Dream in Italian*

I HAVE BEEN A VIRGIL SUAREZ FAN for years now, and this new collection makes this fanboy's heart flutter. In *The Soviet Circus Comes to Havana,* Suarez paints huge, sprawling, lively vistas of life in Havana and expatriate Los Angeles on the miniature canvas of the short story. His stories stretch the frame, overflowing with life, love, comedy, tragedy, and his trademark capacity for burrowing into the human heart. In the hands of a more parsimonious author, any one of the stories in this collection would turn into two or three separate stories, but Virgil Suarez is a generous writer with a wealth of experience to share with us and the uncanny ability to tell it all seamlessly true.

PAT RUSHIN, author of *Puzzling Through the News*

VIRGIL SUAREZ IS ONE OF THE FEW WRITERS out there who can do it all—fiction, nonfiction, poetry. In *The Soviet Circus Comes to Havana and Other Stories,* we are in the presence of a confident writer at the height of his powers. The subtle strands that interweave these stories give this collection the satisfying completeness of a novel. Of the many, many things I admire about Suarez's stories, perhaps foremost is his sublime balance of passion and restraint. He knows when to hit us hard, and he knows when to pull back and let his rich, sensory descriptions do their work. 'I felt it right there,' one of his characters says. Right there—on the body, in the body. The physicality of these stories brings these characters and their worlds to life, whether they're in Los Angeles, Cuba, or Miami. We are always there with them, fighting off demons real and imagined. Such heart, such warmth. Such soul.

JIM DANIELS, author of *Trigger Man*

THIS WONDER-FILLED COLLECTION OF STORIES shows Virgil Suarez joining the ranks of multi-talented writers like Oates and Updike who can produce top work in novels, poems, and short fiction. *The Soviet Circus* stories continually surprise, whether they stem from his boyhood in Cuba or roll knowingly through America, from the West coast to Florida, filled with the tragedies and comedies of unforgettable characters.

PETER MEINKE, author of *The Piano Tuner*

THE SOVIET CIRCUS COMES TO HAVANA
AND OTHER STORIES

The Soviet Circus
Comes to Havana

and other stories

Virgil Suárez

FIRST EDITION

ISBN-13: 978-1-936196-15-9
ISBN-10: 1-936196-15-8
LCCN: 2013950678

Cover design by Harry Pristovnik
Book design by Terrence Chouinard
The typeface used is Haarlemmer.

SOME OF THESE STORIES have appeared or will appear in the following publications, to whose editors grateful acknowledgment is given:

Clackamas Literary Review, Fourteen Hills Literary Review, Green Mountains Review, Gulf Stream, Mid-American Review, New England Review, Ontario Review, Passages North, Patterson Literary Review, Quarterly West, Shenandoah, Takahe (New Zealand), *The Green Hills Literary Lantern, Western Humanities Review, Wascana Review* (Canada), and *Zone 3.*

Several of these stories were nominated by the editors of the magazines in which they first appeared for a Pushcart Prize.

As always, love and thanks to my wife, daughters, and family for their love, good times, food, and conversation.

The work on this book was supported in part by a Florida State Individual Artist Grant.

In Memory of Vance Nye Bourjaily

The Soviet Circus Comes to Havana

ABELARDO and his sister Mirna lived across the street from me in Arroyo Naranjo, Cuba. Abe, as I called him, walked with me to school every day, in the heat of the day, with his impeccable *Pioneritos* school uniform. On the way over, he didn't like to play rough because he said his mother didn't want him to get dirty. This was always the case, and then on the way back we'd wrestle on the grass in the shade of the almond trees that lined the sidewalks of the street we took to go to school.

We removed our red *pañueletas* to wrap rocks in so we could knock down mangoes from the neighbor's yard. Once we had to climb over the fence where there was a dog and Abelardo got his ankle bitten. For a few weeks he didn't walk to school with me, but his sister Mirna did.

She was four years older. She went to a different school, though she too wore a uniform. She didn't say much to me as we walked, but cars would drive by and men would slow down to ask her if she wanted a ride. She never answered them, those men with the shifty eyes, scraggly faces, grease on their hands.

Most of the time they'd slow down and say things to her, like *'Mami, si cocinas como caminas me como hasta tus nalgas.'* Lewd things about her legs, her breasts, what she could do to them with her mouth. These men of missing teeth and yellow-red complexions spoke as if they had a mouth full of food. *If she cooked like she walked, I'd even eat her ass.* That stayed in my mind for days. What did it mean? Mirna herself seemed not to know, or even care.

When she walked next to me she moved with graceful, long strides, her thighs dark and powerful. In the mornings her black hair was wet and combed back over her ears. She looked sleepy, but by the time we got to my school, she often smiled and wished me a good day. Then I watched her walk away.

ABE'S PARENTS moved to the house across the street after the Revolution. His parents were, according to my parents, big Communist Party people, and I believe them because Abe's father drove a Soviet car, a shiny new car he drove up and down the streets of our neighborhood too fast, always honking his horn before pulling into the driveway.

My parents, who were trying to leave the country for the United States, didn't want me to go to the house across the street. They forbade me from doing so. I could play with Abelardo at my house or in the street, but *not* at his house. My father worked at the Hatuey Brewery because the government had placed him there after his arrest. My father had been accused of counter-revolutionary activities by the head of the CDR, *Comite de Defensa y Revolución*. The woman who ran the CDR was good friends with Aberlardo's father, and my father didn't like the connection.

After the brewery job my father was then transferred to the zoo at Lenin's Park. My father was in charge of keeping the big cats well fed. My father spent his days killing horses to feed the lions and tigers, maintaining them in perfect health.

I rarely saw my father during the day, so my mother and grandmother were relaxed about my spending too much time with my *'amiguito comunista,'* as she called Abelardo.

Once his ankle healed and he was able to return to school, we began to walk together again.

'Where is your sister?' I asked him.

'My father drives her to school,' Abe said and smiled as we turned the corner.

I didn't know what to say because though she didn't say much, I liked walking with Mirna. In all her silence she made the walk to school a lot faster. Between the men driving by and shouting nasty words and the way she walked, it seemed to make the trip shorter.

Walking with Abe was a different story. We always had to stop to look at something, be it a crushed snail being devoured by ants, or the time we found a scorpion and he talked me into helping him pick it up and put it in our pencil box until we got home.

Abelardo told me to wait in front of his house and then he ran back out with a can of gasoline. He put the scorpion down, trickled gasoline around it in a small circle before the scorpion could move away, then he searched for something in his pockets.

'What are you doing?' I said.

He brought out a box of matches, lit one, and set the ring on fire.

'Watch,' he said, then squatted for a closer look. I saw the reflection of flames in his hazel eyes. He cracked a wide smile.

The scorpion stopped moving. In a moment's flash the flames consumed it.

'Did you see?' Abelardo said.

'See what?'

'Stung itself.'

I told him the scorpion got burned to a crisp, and it did, turning into a scab-sized curlicue of ash.

'It stung itself,' Abe said and stood up. 'You just didn't see it.'

He told me the next time we caught a scorpion I'd have to pay better attention. The thing stinging itself happened lightning-fast, and when he said 'fast,' he snapped his fingers.

'What are you boys doing?' Mirna's voice came from behind us.

She had been walking down the street toward us and we hadn't noticed.

'Looking at something,' Abe told his sister.

'Don't burn yourselves,' she said and walked right through the gates of her house. Her hair was loose and long. She waved at us without turning back.

Her brother kicked me and said, 'Come on, now that I've got gasoline let's find a lizard.'

I didn't much care to burn things. There was something untrustworthy about fire, I knew, for I had seen one of my cousins get seriously burned when her dress had caught fire. I was there and I watched the fire blacken the dress off her and then burn her skin.

'I better go in,' I said. 'My father'll be home soon.'

'Hey,' Abe shouted at me. 'Does he know when the zoo will reopen?'

I gave him a shrug. I then jumped over the fence of our front yard, went up the steps of our porch, and opened the door. Once inside, I looked out and Abe wasn't in front of his house anymore.

The gate leading up to his house had been left open.

THAT NIGHT, over dinner, my father talked about Lenin's Park. The animals would be ready. Then he told us the story of this terrible thing he'd seen happen to one of the capuchin monkeys. The monkey, tied to a tree nearby but given lots of slack, had learned to climb the Bengal tiger's cage. It would spend days up there taunting the tigers, teasing them with his chain.

Everyday the monkey climbed up there and made fools of those tigers. At first the tigers got taken by the monkey's pirouettes, but then, especially after the tigers ate, they could care less. They'd lay on their sides and sleep away the afternoons. When the monkey made a racket, the tigers didn't even flinch.

Until recently, when there was a food shortage—not enough horses coming in to meat— all the cats grew leaner and hungrier, so one day came while the monkey played on top of the tigers' cage, one of the tigers began to stand and push against the sides of the cage.

My mother and grandmother kept looking at my father to see where this story was going, the way they always looked at him when they wanted him to be aware of his son, me, sitting there listening.

Ah, the eye gesture to let my father know to be careful, no? Would I want to hear such things?

I was transfixed. 'So what happened?' I asked.

'The monkey tripped and fell through the bars.'

'Poor thing,' my grandmother said, of course, as a way to bring closure to the story.

'One tiger grabbed a monkey let, and another tiger the other leg....'

He was chewing fast, my father. I could see he was having a great time sharing this story with us.

'All that was left was the rope dangling there between the bars.'

My grandmother, her white shiny hair catching the light of the dining room lamp, rolled her eyes.

At school Abe and I sat nearby in class, though I had the spot nearest the window. I liked looking out the window, especially when it started to pour and I could see the flag high up on the poll get soaked so that it wouldn't fly. For days it would hang there limp, and it reminded me of the monkey's rope and my father's story.

It had been too long since I'd seen Abe's sister. I kept writing her name in the back of my notebook in cursive, with each letter turning in wide-eye loops. I drew roots on the feet of the 'M.' Once Abe leaned over to spy on what I was doing, but I caught him in time and closed my notebook.

Our teacher, *Compañera* Garcia, was a short, no-neck woman who wore a too-tight green uniform. Her sweat made dark crescents under the armpits of her shirts.

'*Compañero* Suárez,' she said slithering the 's' and 'z' in my name, for emphasis, of course. 'We know you are leaving the country,' she said, 'but until then could you pay attention. You might just learn something.'

Paying attention meant looking toward the front the classroom where the pictures of the *barbudos*—as my grandmother called Fidel, Camilo, and Che—hung. The bearded heroes of the Revolution. They looked like my uncles, so I was not impressed. My uncles riding in on their horses from the rice fields.

There used to be a map of our island with the tip of Florida just peeking above it, but that map was replaced by a big one of our island, filled with these little red stars and circles of the great battles and victories of the Revolution.

'Next week,' *Compañera* Garcia told us, 'we are going to study our victory at Playa Girón over the Yankee Imperialists.'

Abe loved to hear stories of wars and battles, so he salivated at the prospect of hearing more about the Bay of Pigs Invasion. He drew tanks and rifles on his notebooks. Soon we'd be taking classes on how to dismantle and reassemble AK-47s. This would be an integral part of our graduation.

This was one reason why my parents were desperate to take me out of the country, because all this talk of war and fighting in far-away countries scared them. My father said we were not communists and we would never be, so even when he had to call people compañe-ro, which was Spanish for 'comrade,' he turned red and could hardly swallow right.

At the end of class, right before we were about to stand and salute the flag and the pictures of our leaders, *Compañera* Garcia told us about Lenin's Park and the zoo's grand opening.

'Long live Vladimir Lenin!' she commanded us to repeat.

'Long live Lenin!' we shouted back.

'Long live Karl Marx!' she barked from the front of the room.

'Long live Marx!'

'Long live Fidel!' With Fidel she really belted it out, as she expected us to.

'LONG LIVE FIDEL!'

I thought the shouting would bring the walls down, or at least that map of our solitary island floating away into a blue expanse.

THE ZOO was about to open. Abe and I were really excited, though we both knew he'd get there first. The opening day was strictly for Party people and their families, for CDR families, and for people who were good comrades and had volunteered lots of their time to cutting sugar cane, harvesting potatoes, picking coffee.

Abe told me his father said there'd be a rally and a demonstration with planes flying over, *paracaidistas* (parachutes), mock-battle sce-narios—the works. And I would miss it. I could tell from the sound of his voice he enjoyed bragging like this. But he was my friend and I liked hanging out with him.

'My father's going to take me,' I said.

'Has he gotten tickets?' Abe asked.

'I don't know. But we are going.'

'We have the best seats,' he said.

We were playing marbles until I started beating him and he got bored. He put the few he had left back in his pockets and told me his parents were not at home.

'You want to see my room?' he said.

Then I remembered what my parents said.

'Sure,' I said.

We ran inside and I followed him.

'I can't stay long,' I said.

Abe ran fast. He could run faster than me. He came from an athletic family. His parents were both tall, slim, fit. Must be all that marching and rallying they did at Plaza José Martí, where Fidel gave his long speeches.

I ran after Abe, up the front porch steps, past the rocking chairs by the columns of the porch and inside the house. The furniture looked old and heavy, passed down from generations.

I remembered my mother telling me stories of the rich people who'd lived in the house before and how they disappeared. It happened all the time, my mother said, and then a new family moved in.

'This way,' Abe said. He ran up a flight of stairs making loud thumping noises with his school shoes on the parquet floors.

I followed him inside his room. There were posters of movie stars and baseball players and boxers. He had a signed poster of Teofilo Stevens, the hero of Cuban boxing, the man who always brought home the gold from the Olympics.

Plastic cars and dolls lined his bookshelves. I couldn't believe it, and he never once brought one out. Instead we were setting things on fire with gasoline, or shooting rocks at birds. I had always wondered how deep his marble supply was, and now I knew. There was a big water dispenser-sized jug full of them. They shone through the thick glass of the container. I wanted to reach my hand in all the way to my elbow and grab handfuls.

Abe stuck his arm under his bed and pulled out a magazine. It was wrapped in a towel. When he unwrapped the bundle, I saw the stack of model train catalogues. I focused on the writing, but I couldn't make it out.

'My father returned from Germany,' Abe said, 'and brought me these.'

I saw the pictures of the little towns and trains riding through them. The down-to-size scale people and animals.

'He says he is going to bring me a set next time.'

I burned with jealousy. I could feel my ears and cheeks getting hot.

Why was he getting these things? Why did Abe have a father who traveled to other countries and brought him back all these goodies?

He took the shiny, glossy-paged catalogues from my hands, re-wrapped them in the towels, and put them under his bed.

'Why do you keep them there?' I asked.

He shrugged. 'My secret,' he said. 'My sister and mom don't know. Hey, you want some lemonade?'

'I better get going,' I said.

At that very moment the front door slammed shut, and we heard footsteps coming up the stairs. Heavy footsteps.

Abe peeked out and then said, 'Ah, it's my sister.'

'Stay here,' he said and left.

I reached under the bed, unwrapped the bundle and held those catalogues again. I paged through one and gazed at the locomotives, the cattle wagons, the red and yellow cabooses. The layouts of toy trains passing through marvelous cities and little towns with rivers and bridges.

The door was open wide and there stood Mirna. She was as surprised as I was. I guess she was expecting to find her brother.

She stood in the doorway in shorts and a blouse, the hallway light coming from behind her, her hair catching some of its radiance.

'Oh,' she said. 'Where is Abe?'

I slid the catalogues back under the bed and pretended this sort of thing happened to us all the time, me being in her house, and she walking into her brother's room barefoot, holding the door open with her manicured and painted nails.

'He went to get us lemonade.'

I stood and leaned against the dresser where I almost toppled over a toy robots.

'Are you going to the opening of Lenin's Park?' she asked.

'Sure,' I said.

'I'm not.' I watched her lips move as she stressed the 'not.' 'It's going to be boring. Too many people.'

'But it's the circus,' I said.

'Who cares about a bunch of Russian clowns,' she said and smiled.

Abe returned with two glasses of lemonade, pushed her sister out of the way and handed me a glass.

Refrigerator, I thought as I took the glass. Cold. They had a refrigerator that worked.

I began to drink my lemonade. Stopped when Mirna left the room, and swigged down the rest in one gulp.

'Gotta go,' I said, and walked out of his room, down the hallway past Mirna's room. Her door was closed, but I could see light coming through underneath.

Down the stairs and out of the house. I was breathless when I made it to the front gate and the commotion of people gathering on the sidewalk. Up ahead I heard trumpets and horns, and drumming. The clash of cymbals. There were lots of people. Everybody in the neighborhood had come out to watch the parade of the Soviet Circus.

Waves of people everywhere. Workers, police, mothers and their babies. They cheered and whistled.

I saw my mother and grandmother across the street, they were waving me over, their hands saying 'hurry, hurry,' over the lines of people gathered there to watch.

'The Soviet Circus Visits Havana,' read my father in *Granma*, the Cuban paper.

My mother told him all about the parade when he came home from work.

Over dinner he made an announcement. It was settled. My father was taking me to the circus. My grandmother didn't want to go, and my mother warned my father to be careful, not to let me out of his sight.

When the day came, we headed out early that afternoon, after my father returned from work. I dressed in my long pants, and a short-sleeved shirt because my mother said it'd be very hot.

At Lenin's park my father and I walked across the railroad tracks circling the park, across an overgrown field of grass, by a lake bank where the amphitheater was being built, to the entrance of the park where they pitched tents. In the wind the tents looked like a giant's green belly.

I stared and the tents from where we were asked to make a long line to get in. My father looked around to see how far out we were. We didn't want to miss the show.

I thought of Abe and his father, who had arrived a few days earlier, without the hassle of lines and given cotton candy, popcorn, chocolate bars—anything they wanted.

I heard all about how great it had been. The magic show. The trapeze act. The clowns. The trained elephants.

By the time we made it inside the three-ring tent, I was tired. My father held on to me with sweaty hands. It was a muggy night in Havana.

There were people everywhere. Most of them in foul moods.

Next to us a man and woman kept arguing, the din of their voices rising above the piped in music. The man kept calling the woman a liar, and the woman kept calling the man a *comemierda,* an idiot.

When the man saw that I was paying attention, he turned to the woman and said, *'Fiñe,'* which I did not know until many years later that it was just another word for a kid, *un chamaco.* But it took me by surprised then because I thought they had seen something in my stare.

We took our seats in the back row of bleachers because my father was a dissident and, as such, we couldn't sit up front with my schoolmates.

The lights finally dimmed, there was a blackout, and then they came up again. The Russian clowns emerged, marching around the stage in glittering sequin uniforms, frowns on their painted faces, plastic AK-47s over their shoulders.

Then they were making funny noises, some kind of racket from down below. People got up in the rows in front of us. I couldn't see. My father urged people to sit down so that we could see, too.

There were one-legged unicyclists in puffy outfits, orange hair, red noses that sounded like car horns when another clown pinched them. Each cyclist struggled to keep from falling. If he fell off, he'd get trampled by the elephants in their camouflaged banners that read *Cuba y La Union Sovietica, Patria o Muerte!*

The big animals blew their trunks, stormed about like tanks, defecated in big piles on the hay on the stage floor. Sweepers in uniforms with bumble bee stripes swept up the paddies. Jugglers tossed what looked like human heads up in the air.

I couldn't see very well. I was exhausted from hours of standing.

'The heads,' someone said, 'of *gusanos.*'

Gusano was what other men called my father, our family. It meant dissident. It was not a nice name. I would have settled for *comemierda*, but who wanted to be called a maggot? The tongue in each mouth of the tossed heads stuck out in mock slobber. Each man had confessed too much, somebody turned around and said to my father.

A lion tamer in tight General's pants whipped the big cats into a frenzied revolutionary song. My father carried me up high on his shoulders, tall and proud—above us the trapeze artists fell, plummeting, one after another, like big fish on a billowed safety net. The crowd cheered.

I didn't get it. I felt repulsed. The people in the stands had had enough too. They began to boo. What kind of a circus was this?

Someone shouted: 'Propaganda bullshit!'

The riot police responded by releasing rainbow-colored canisters of tear gas. They fired rubber bullets up in the air, then shouted in Russian for everyone to go home, *a la casa.*

At that moment the armless tightrope walker lost his balance, grabbed on to the rope with his teeth.

He bit hard, hanging on.

One of the knife-throwers aimed and struck him down.

My father pulled me out of there fast. In the waves of people pushing and running out for air, I lost a shoe. I kept knocking against peoples' backs and arms and hands. My father said something about a fight. I couldn't hear him.

He kept tugging at me, hurting my arm because he didn't want to let go. I held on to his lose shirt, my hands sweaty and slippery.

Once we were out of there, we hurried home. I began to limp. When my father saw that I had lost a shoe, he picked me up and perched me on his shoulders. It was a long way home.

Eventually he would carry me in his arms. I kept thinking of Mirna's words about the circus. I knew our days in Havana were numbered.

As my father carried me back home in his arms, I fell asleep listening to his quickened breathing, his heartbeats like the hooves of those Russian elephants, the dashed hopes of a *gusano,* and his son.

The Delgado's Son

THE THREE TIMES my parents visited, they took me with them to visit the Delgado's, a friend of my father's from Hatuey Brewery where they worked the bottle-checking lines. My father took me there once, and I watched as the empty bottles passed in front of a lit screen, and my father sat there inspecting them for defects in the glass, a broken rim, a fleck of something inside. Blemishes. Spots. My father kept a collection of these strange, defective bottles under his stool and work desk. He showed me the broken bottles. The ones with pieces of insects, the hair-line fractures. Simply the bottles that didn't look right. I held a couple, looked at them in the light, and I really couldn't figure out what was wrong. I guessed that's why they needed somebody like my father checking, double checking, just to be sure. On the other side worked Carlos Delgado, my father's friend, who'd stick out his purplish tongue at me, a wisp of his salt and pepper hair falling in front of his face. My father said that Carlos had never cut his hair, some kind of promise he'd made a long time ago. The Delgado's were devotees of San Lázaro, one of Cuba's major saints.

At his house when you walked in, they had a life-sized statue of San Lázaro, the leper, with replicas of the dogs licking his festering wounds around the old man's legs. The crutches were real wood crutches, armpit pads and all, and the old man's eyes followed you as you entered. The dogs' too. At least the one dog that wasn't constantly licking. The statue stood on a small circumference of cement inside a large pond where Carlos kept goldfish. The fish came up in a flash of orange and ivory, gulped down air and dove to the black depth of the pond. Ferns grew all around the periphery of the pond, feather smooth, flecked with seeds the size of pinheads underneath each leaf. The pond I liked, the statue and the dogs I found creepy. The three times we visited I only tried to look at the fish, not at the old man looking down at me.

My parents insisted that I accompany them whenever I visited because they said the Delgados liked me. Mrs Delgado always fed me these squared pieces of *melcocha*, a candy made out of pure brown sugar, or *boniatillo* made from sweet yams. My favorite was *raspacoco* made with coconut, hard on the teeth, extra sweet on the tongue. The first time Bertha, as Mrs Delgado liked to be called, *'con la hache,'* as she always said, 'Bert-*hache*-a,' took me to the kitchen where I saw their altar to Santa Barbara, another Afro-Cuban deity.

On the altar there were candles, food, necklaces, red goblets full of *centavos,* Cuban pennies. She saw me looking and asked me, *'¿Es linda, verdad?'* Isn't she pretty?

I nodded my head yes, though again I couldn't bring myself to look at the Virgin's sad, porcelain-glossy eyes. They kept following me. Bertha was a short woman, with black hair and thick legs. She wore an amulet around her right ankle. It was made from red and black beads the size of coffee beans. What I liked about Mrs Delgado, other than her sweet, delicious candies, were her hands. She had these small, perfectly manicured hands, ivory moons polished on each fingernail. I looked at them each time she gave me something to eat. She made lemonade too. They had a lemon tree in their back yard.

After our first visit, I pretended to fall asleep in my father's arm as he and my mother walked back home from Carlos' and Bertha's house, and I heard my mother kid my father about his liking Bertha. I almost said I liked her too, but then I remembered I was pretending to be asleep because, although I was almost eight, I loved to be carried in my father's arms.

That first time we visited the Delgado's home, and I was in the kitchen waiting for Bertha to reach to the cabinet and hand me the surprise treat, I heard the scratching on the door. I noticed Bertha stop in mid-opening of the cabinet door, and she looked at me and smiled. I thought it was the sound a cat makes trying to get inside the kitchen. Then the scratching stopped and I thought I heard a hum.

That's when Bertha starting asking me questions in a fairly loud tone. I thought she merely wanted for my parents to hear us in the kitchen. I don't know exactly why I thought that, but I did right there, standing close enough to her to smell the aroma of her perfume.

'How's school?' she asked.

I said, 'Fine.'

'You have friends?'

'A couple,' I answered.

'What do you learn, at school?'

'History. Science. Math.'

'Are you learning about Che and Camilo?'

Che and Camilo were revolutionary heroes in 1969, our last year in Cuba, the year we visited the Delgado's three times. 'Yes,' I said, 'and Fidel too.'

'*¿Y qué más?*' she asked, handing me a couple of treats.

I held one in my hands, and the other automatically went to my mouth. Soft *melcocha,* so sweet it made the words stick to the back of my throat, the walls of my mouth.

Suddenly, she took me out of the kitchen, and we returned to the living room where my parents sat with Carlos. They were drinking rum. I could smell it on my father's breath. My mother didn't like for my father to drink too much because he'd start talking about the is-land's situation, *la situación del país,* and about his wanting to get out, leave. The walls have ears is what my grandmother always said, and my mother liked to tell that to my father.

'Carlos and I are good buddies, right, Carlos?' my father would says.

'*Claro que sí, compay,*' Carlos would say and smile, then take a sip from his watermelon-print glass.

I was chewing on the delicious *melcocha,* listening to my parents talk with the Delgados. I kept looking all around at their heavy, brown furniture, the big, glossy floor tiles, the sound of the fish coming up for gulps of air coming from the pond, the miniature soldiers Carlos collected in a line behind a glass cabinet. I loved those soldiers, Roman gladiators, the Royal Chinese Guards, the Egyptians next to the scaled-down Sphinx, Napoleon's armies at Waterloo. Carlos always promised to open the cabinet and show them to me up close, but each time he'd try to do it, Bertha would pull him away. I would stay there looking at realistic *maquetas,* as Carlos called these battle scenes he made and painted.

In another cabinet he put together airplane models. He told my father putting them together eased the tension in his hands, kept his mind off other things, if he knew what Carlos meant. My father'd laugh at this and remind his friend he wasn't a surgeon. Both men would laugh as though they were already drunk.

'No soy cirujano,' Carlos would say and tremble with laughter so much his glasses would slide down the bridge of his nose, his hair would fall in front of his eyes, the way it did when he sat behind the light checking defects in bottles.

If it weren't for the fact that I loved to look at the soldiers and the model planes, I would have asked my parents to leave me at home with my grandmother who read to me stories from *Arabian Nights.* My favorite story out of that book was the story of Ali Baba and the Forty Thieves. I liked the way my grandmother pronounced '¡Abrete Sésamo!'

DURING our second visit, Carlos almost opened the cabinet where he kept his miniature soldiers. I could almost touch one when Bertha pulled him away to the kitchen. For the first time I realized that perhaps I'd never hold one of those figurines (and to this day I still wondered if my parents knew what was going on) when they kept doing that: Bertha taking Carlos to the kitchen, asking my parents for *disculpa.* 'Discúlpanos, Suárez,' that's what Bertha would tell my parents, and then they'd both disappear to the kitchen.

Of course each time this happened, Bertha would return with tall, iced glasses of lemonade and more candies, cookies, little *pastelitos* she said she'd learned to make from her mother's recipe, her mother, bless her soul. *Guayaba* or mango pastries.

It was during that second visit, while Bertha and Carlos were in the kitchen, and my parents sitting in the living room, that I came very close to turning the cabinet's key and touching one of the soldiers, this Roman lashing four horses, two white and two black, pulling a golden chariot. The horses in the front had their front hooves lifted, giving them a fiery, bestial expression.

I was almost there when the screaming started. It sounded like the shrieking of a parrot or some animal coming from the kitchen. I turned the key to lock the cabinet and returned to my parents' side. They sat there as though they hadn't heard what I'd heard, my father sipping his lemonade, my mother looking at a *Bohemia* magazine.

I wanted to asked them if they had heard what I had. But I felt guilty for having almost opened the cabinet.

The screaming grew louder, a door opened, slammed shut. More screaming, then I heard Carlos pleading with someone in another room. Clearly, he said 'No' three times. The last 'NO!' really resounded in the living room, and then everything returned to the usual silence.

My father sipped his lemonade.

My mother turned another page.

Bertha came back in to the living room and joined my mother on the sofa. 'Anything good,' she asked my mother.

My mother shook her head no.

Soon Carlos returned too, his hair brushed back. He sat down with my father, and they started talking about the old days, when they both rode around on horseback, when they went fishing and hunting in Ciénega de Zapata. The turtles, the fish they caught, the cayman they killed.

On the way home that night, I walked between my parents. There was a city-wide blackout to save energy. At least that's the way our teacher explained it to us at school. In times of scarcity, the whole island needed to save energy. Who knew when the *Yanquis*...that's what they called *Los Americanos,* people from the United States. *Los Yan-*

quis Imperialistas. The water would go out too, which used to infuriate my grandmother. The only times I heard her curse were when the water got turned off.

'What happened?' I asked my parents as we all walked in the moonlight. There was a gentle breeze blowing in from shore. I heard it in the trees.

'Where?' my mother asked.

I asked about what had happened earlier. *Los gritos,* I said. The screaming.

My mother turned to my father and looked at him. Then they both looked down at me.

'The screaming?'

Come on, I thought, *surely you guys must have heard it too.*

'Do they have parrot?' I asked.

'No parrots,' my father said.

'A dog?'

'No dog.'

'A cat?'

'No cat.'

DURING the third and final visit—it'd be the last visit for me, for I can't recall ever hearing my parents say they returned to the Delgado's house after the fact—I sat next to my mother on the sofa so that when the screaming started again, I'd nudge her on the side or pull on her skirt to let her know to listen.

After we entered and walked beyond the deep-set, following eyes of San Lázaro and his spooky, mangy dogs, we sat down in the living room. Carlos and Bertha, dressed up in pressed clothes, stood there by their furniture as though they had come back from a party or some place in Old Havana where they'd gone to dance or to the movies. They looked very made up.

My parents and the Delgados always talked about the American movies, their favorite movie stars of the 50s and 60s. My father always brought up John Wayne, my mother her favorite of all time, Robert Mitchum in *Cape Fear*. Bertha adored Victor Mature, and Carlos always said he liked the comedians like Charlie Chaplin, *El flaco y el gordo* (Laurel and Hardy), and Jimmy Durante. He made fun of Jimmy Durante's nose. But nobody could compare to Humphrey Bogart in *Casablanca* or *The Maltese Falcon*. '*Ese ameircano es un bárbaro*.'

I was waiting for a lull in the conversation to lure Carlos back to the miniature cabinet when the ruckus began in the back room. Both Carlos and Bertha got up at the same time and ran to the kitchen. There must have been a back room somewhere, someone kicking at the door, pounding with both fists on wood, kicking and screaming.

'That noise,' I said to my parents. 'You hear it now?'

They both sat there quietly, turning their ears the way dogs do when they hear a strange sound.

'Sure,' my father said.

'I hear it too,' said my mother and sat up on the sofa.

Suddenly a door whipped open and a naked, pink-fleshed boy ran out toward us. His skin glowed, I swore. A red birthmark splotched on his back, the size of a sparrow. Purplish-red toward the edges.

My father stood up as though the boy wasn't a boy but a bull charging at him. The boy, tongue sticking out of his mouth, long haired, naked from head to foot, jumped on the sofa next to my mother, rubbed himself against her, grabbed her head and kissed her.

My father and I sat there stunned.

The bug-eyed boy had a hard and erect penis. Thin and arched like a dog's. He held it and rubbed it, stuck a finger in his mouth.

It's hard to say how much time passed between the boy's explosive attack on my mother and us in the living room, and Carlos' running around after the boy whom he finally tackled, fell on him on the floor, wrapped the boy's arms around so he couldn't moved, lifted him up, naked and pink, into his arms and ran him out of the room.

Bertha stood back right below the frame of the kitchen door, below the replica of '*Ultima Cena de Jesús Cristo*' and his twelve disciples. Crying, she held herself steady as her husband stormed passed her.

Carlos' hair came undone and he looked like a beast himself as he carried the boy out of sight. Then more screaming and banging. A door slamming shut, locking. A silence so deep we stood there shaking in its wake.

My mother and father stood up to go. I followed them to the door. My father stopped by the front door, right there by San Lázaro, his dogs, the goldfish coming up for air. I don't know what they were expecting. Maybe Carlos and Bertha to appear and say how sorry they were. *La disculpa.*

I turned to look at the statue's eyes following us out the door.

We closed the door between us, and I never saw the Delgados again. On the way home my father told my mother that everyone in Cuba, everyone he knew, had secrets, but nothing like this.

I walked a little behind them. The moon was still full. The stars blinked and shone, cloistered in corners of the dark sky. It was a hot night. I kept replaying the scene, the boy storming into the living room, not wanting to believe in it, the soldiers in the cabinet keeling over from the vibrations on the wood floor. The birthmark on his back opening like the wings of a bird. His erect penis like a flower in his hands.

For days and nights I daydreamed and had nightmares like what must have spooked that Roman soldier's chariot horses, the black ones rearing back on their legs, neighing at the precipice, some unknown that held them back in this life.

Like the Delgado's son still screaming from that locked, back room of their house in Old Havana.

The Initiation

GROWING UP an only son in Arroyo Naranjo, Cuba, I heard via my schoolmates of the gang on our street, *Los Corsarios Negros,* who hung out at the corner long after us young ones were in bed, under the billowed mosquito netting—I could hear them at the corner, their chatting like the sound of cicadas during the day, right before it rained.

Sometimes I heard them break glass bottles, or pop these tiny bombs I learned to make later out of two screws and a thick nut, inside as many match heads as I could grind—and they'd be tossed up into the air and if it landed on either screw head, it'd pop. Pop. Sometimes loud enough startle my grandmother in the other room, and she would tell my father who would then step out onto the porch and shout at the boys at the corner.

Nobody really knew who belonged to the gang, but I heard rumors at school.

Fermin—the black kid who sat behind me in class and who also ate my pencil erasers as fast as the teacher gave them to me—told me that half of the class was in the gang. I looked around at all the other kids, dressed like me in their blue shirts, red *pañueleta* around their necks, their hair combed neatly, cut short, like mine, scalloped at the front— the classic *malanguita*, as my father always said to the barber. No, I couldn't or rather wouldn't believe it. If some of these fools, I thought, could be in the gang, so could I. It would be my secret.

At home I told my best friend Ricardito, who lived at the corner of the block, right next to us, but he was too afraid. Lanky and tall, he was a bit awkward, uncoordinated. When we rode bikes, he fell. If we skated, he always skinned his elbows and knees. No, he'd have no part of it. On the playground one day I approached three boys, all taller and bigger than me, and I simply asked what it took to be part of the gang— the infamous *Corsarios*. I thought of pirates because my grandmother had read to me stories of pirates in the port of New Orleans, always making the stories sound exotic, far, far away—I love those stories.

The Black Corsairs, who roamed the Havana nights pulling pranks, breaking windows, deflating car tires... the mischief was endless. The three boys eyed me as though I had asked them something in Greek or Chinese. They looked beyond me at the teachers keeping vigil on the playground—and I remember the day, one of those radiant Havana days, not a cloud in the sky, a warm breeze making the almond tree leaves flicker and reflect the sunlight, like hands waving—and the boys took me aside and asked me where I had heard of the gang. They told me I could only join if I promised not to ever utter the name of the gang, which I did immediately in my head: *Los Corsarios Negros. Shhh. Shhh.*

They told me to meet them tonight at the corner of Balmaseda and Luz, that I had to sneak out and meet them there at the corner. All day I kept planning how I would sneak out of the house. My parents always listened to music on the radio late into the evening, after dinner, with my grandmother talking about the old days, so I couldn't leave through the front door. The back door my mother always locked and then stacked a whole bunch of pots and pans—her own *alarma,* she called it, meaning if someone opened the door they'd be ruckus so loud it would wake us all up, and then? *'Entonces?'* my father always asked and smiled.

Before I was born he had been a policeman and rumor had it he still had his gun. In all the hours I spent snooping around in drawers and behind the furniture, I never found it, but I heard two of my uncles who visited us talking about it. My father didn't have it anymore because when he stopped being a policeman, he gave it back. My parents wanted to leave the country, my father that same year of *Los Corsarios Negros* had announced it to my mother's huge family. Very few people were happy about it, but my father said he mostly worried about my future, how they needed to get me out of Cuba before I was in scripted into the army.

I thought of another way of getting out of the house, sneak out of my room. I knew how to remove the glass panes of the window—they had a latch, and I could remove the slats one by one, all I needed to do was to remove four of them. At seven, I was a small, skinny kid—one of my uncles called me *El Maja*, which I learned later was a joke in reference to Goya's 'La Maja.' But *El Maja* meant a kind of Cuban snake, very common in our backyards.

I once killed one by the rabbit cages with my father's machete. It rose up as if to bite me, and I swung and chopped its head clean off. The rest of it I watch wiggle and form these small and big Ss. So that's what I would do, I thought. I would remove the window slats, and jump out the window. Then I thought of the chickens my father kept corralled on that side of the house—what if I startled them in their sleep and they'd start to cackle? I would slither out, I told myself, after all, I was *El Maja* about to join *Los Corsarios Negros*.

THAT NIGHT, with a great deal of anticipation, I ate all my food, washed up and told my parents I was going to bed—even my grandmother looked at me and then asked if I felt okay. I simply told them what I had prepared, I was very tired. It'd been a long day at school, which was partly true because they had made us march in unison around the flag pole, stop, sing the national anthem, march more, stop, sing, march, stop, sing, march—we were going to be taken on a field trip to Plaza de la Revolucion in Havana, where *El Maximo Lider* was going to give a speech, like those I had stayed up with my parents (and falling asleep throughout) in front of the television, which only seemed to work when there were rallies and speeches.

While my parents cleaned up the table and then came to the living room to chat, I removed the glass vanes of the window very slowly. One by one. I kept checking on the chickens right outside the window. I kept going *ssh-ssh,* just to get them used to the small noises and sounds I would be making, if I had to make any noise at all. By the third slat removed, I knew I could sneak out. The fourth one I placed on my mattress, and then placed my pillow on top of it. I clambered out and sure enough, some of the chickens got startled by they didn't make a sound.

I climbed on top of the henhouse, then on to the cement fence right by Ricardito's bedroom window, and from there on to the roof, as I had done during the days when I went up on the roof to play, pretend I was a pilot in the air force, knocking down the yellowed coconuts off the palm trees on our front yard. I was like a cat, already I felt proud that I was almost going to be a *Corsario.*

Once on top of the roof, I went around toward the corner, making sure not to catch one of my shoe laces on a roof tile and fall—I didn't want Manuel or Josefina waking up, if they were sleeping. Like my parents they were probably listening to the radio too. They didn't have a television and that's how me and Ricardito became such good friends. He was always over to watch the cartoons like Porky Pig and Mighty Mouse.

ONCE at the corner, I jumped onto a tall papaya tree and slid down, scraping my forearms a little, but I didn't care. I was ready for more.

The corner was really dark, the boys had already knocked out the lights. I didn't hear anything at all. The whole street was dark, and I could see a couple of *cucuyos,* the fireflies, flickering across the street by the corner trash dump. I waited, and nothing. I started to bite my fingernails, feeling quite nervous and excited. (To this day I still bite my nails.)

I waited what felt like all night and nobody came. I watched my own shadow, and then I started to get afraid, and just when I was about to leave, I heard the sound of a car speeding down the street, and in fact a black car drove passed me, turned at the corner, and then it stopped in front of my house. I heard its door open. I walked closer and saw two men getting out of the car.

What kind of trouble was I in? I couldn't help but imagine. I hurried around the back, jumped over two fences—couldn't climb on the roof again, but I came in through the back of our house, jumped a smaller chain-linked fence, and just as I was climbing back into my room, I heard the knock on the door.

One heave and I climbed up on to the windowsill, my elbows scraping on the wall. I felt the rough edges cut my skin. My grandmother turned off the radio and once I was back in my room, I heard my mother whisper something or other to my father. The men, she said, were G–2. Special police agents. Secret police.

They wanted to speak with my father at the station. I heard my father go to the door. I stepped on to the bed, having forgotten the vane on the mattress, and I broke it. I heard it snap like a bone under my foot. I jumped down in time to hear one of the men tell my father he had to accompany them. I heard my mother's voice crackle with concern.

'No,' she told my grandmother. '*Se llevan a Villo, Isabel.*' My grandmother told my mother to go with my father. They took her too. My grandmother locked the door behind them, and then I heard her in the kitchen. She opened the faucet but there was no sound of water. I came out of the room.

She saw that I was dressed, notice too my bleeding elbows and forearms.

'*Que te paso, niño?*' she asked me.

I wanted to know what was going on with my father.

She asked me what I was doing dressed.

She took a dishrag and wet it, brought it over and cleaned the blood off my elbows, my arms, my fingers.

I was not going anywhere.

I asked about my parents. Where did they go? Not to worry, my grandmother told me, that they'd be right back.

She came to my bedroom and helped me take off my clothes, to get back in bed. When she pulled the sheet and the pillow, she saw the broken glass. I explained it to her. She didn't understand, but she had more on her mind.

The gaping hole on my window she could deal with later, but my parents absence. It made her shake. She changed the sheet where there were pieces of glass, then she put me to bed. She kept me company long after both of our hearts had quieted. I could still hear mine on my pillow.

The house was dark.

I heard the chickens flinch on their perches.

No other sounds.

The mosquito netting hung above us, enveloped us like an open mouth.

Then I asked my grandmother, who was holding my hand real tight, to tell me another story starring *Los Corsarios Negros* of New Orleans.

Blown

YOU COME to the Toucan Club on Sunset Boulevard to sober up.

This is the best place in Los Angeles where you can sit and relax and listen to Latin jazz. Your favorite hang out. Something about the lights swirling, these blurs and flashes against the smooth, shiny surfaces. A constant clink of glass, voices talking, laughter, good times, what the living must do.

The girl you are with, Carla, wants to go someplace else, but you're too tired and strung out to keep partying. Not much conversation between you two, but she keeps asking for the little plastic bag and running to the bathroom to do a couple more lines.

Her nervousness is annoying. Or is it her greed? She blows coke like she does everything else, with complete abandon. Maybe it bothers you because you hate to be alone. It's when you find yourself alone that you start to think about all the things you don't want to think about, like war, bad marriages, children who no longer speak to their fathers. You used to be an asshole, but living into your forties mellows everyone out.

THE BAND comes back, these five guys in tropical carnival-type outfits, from a break and picks up their instruments. Some of their songs are new, which makes you wonder how long it's been since the last time you were here. The waitress keeps returning to your table to clean the ashtray, replace the hot sauce or corn chips. Each time she makes conversation. Something you appreciate. Her hair is tied into a pony tail, a turquoise band holding it back. Very nice. She tells you the place is hopping tonight. She likes it when it is this crowded. More tips, more conversation. More electricity. She's been bringing you stiff drinks, double alcohol. You think she likes you.

For these reasons, you think, you'll leave her a Benjamin Franklin.

Carla walks back to the table quickly, trying not to stagger. Braless, her small round breasts bounce under the silk of her V-shaped, white dress, her nipples dark as pennies, erect. There's a birthmark on her right breast, you remember, which darkens when her nipples become aroused.

'Ordered you another White Russian,' you say, reaching over and wiping her upper lip with your thumb. She's twenty-two, a college student drop-out turned court stenographer. For someone who spends her days taking words down, she hardly talks.

'Can't handle it,' she says, handing you the bag under the table.

'Drink coffee.'

'Coffee and coke don't mix,' she says, then puts her house keys into her leather purse.

'Sure they do.'

'Coke and holy water don't.'

'You mean 'fire' water.' *Aguardiente.* Rot-gut stuff.

You check the Ziplock with your finger to make sure that the bag is sealed, then drop it into your shirt pocket without looking at the bag.

'Any left?' you say.

'Enough to get us home.' She says and cuts a smile.

She lives like this most of her days. She lives in Glendale with two cats and a Chihuahua who keeps chewing the leather of your shoes, tucking them under the bed. At night you don't go to the bathroom because you don't want to step on it by accident, don't want to hear the yawp-yawp and door scratching. Her mother is dead. Her father is dead. No brothers or sisters. She's as alone as you are.

But you like the way she looks, firm arms and thighs, strong abdomen, her cut-short hair. The way she pronounces each word as though she's got something sweet in her mouth.

Like now when she says home.

The way she pronounces home makes you think of what the two of you'll do there. More liquor, of course. And coke, to speed things up. In the bedroom you'll watch her undress, slip the g-string undies slowly, knowing you are watching. The smooth skin of her back.

The waitress brings the drinks and sets them away from your hands. She's still smiling. You take a sip of your Remy Martin and hold it in your mouth for a while, then swallow it quickly. The waitress wipes the ashtray clean, picks up her tray and leaves.

'Let's toast to life,' you say, raising your glass.

'Fuck life,' Carla says, 'keep inventing stories.'

This is what she calls you opening up, revealing a few things about your life, like the times you lived in Cuba. How you got out.

'Toast to that,' you say.

'And to whatever's left in your pocket.'

This is what you see when you look at the mirrored wall behind Carla: a pale face, not too-bad of a receding hair line, yours swept back by the wind from driving your convertible Spitfire, and narrow eyes too distant for you to see how utterly bloodshot they are.

'I bet you didn't know I was in Vietnam,' you say.

'A Cuban in Vietnam?'

You notice how her fingers shake as she takes a cigarette out of the YSL Ritz pack.

'When the time came, everybody went,' you say.

'Not everybody.'

'You were here?' you ask.

'Cuba,' she says and looks at the man playing the electric piano. He jumps up and down as he starts his solo.

'Like I said, I went.'

'All right,' she says. 'How many did you kill?'

'I got there at the end. Before I knew it I was back.'

'That's anti-climactic.'

'So what.'

'You saw no action over there?'

'You know, the usual. Helicopters airlifting the wounded. Huts fire-bombed to ashes. Some bombing.'

'And nothing happened to you?'

'Not a scratch,' you say. You take a cigarette and light it.

'I can't believe it.' You can smell what people are drinking, smoking around you. So much perfume, enough to make you feel light-headed.

'Documentary footage stuff. That's it.'

You blow smoke into her face.

There is a moment of silence between songs when you have to lower your voice.

'I don't like the way you make it sound,' Carla says. The way she stares at your fingers makes you wish you knew what she is thinking about.

'I'll spare you the details.'

She crushes the cigarette on the ashtray, then finishes whatever is left of her drink.

You continue: 'See, I attend these group sessions at the VA hospital. The government pays for it, so I go.'

'In other words,' she says, 'you're abusing—'

'Let me finish,' you say, 'they think I'm fucked in the head like most of these other guys in there.'

'There's nothing wrong with you,' she says, then begins to laugh.

'I love going to the meetings. That's how I find out what I missed. Some of these guys tell great stories. Sometimes they piss me off because they don't want to believe I was there.'

'I believe you.'

'Something funny happened during one of the meetings. I can't remember what I was trying to say but I got so frustrated I stood up and clapped my hands.'

You clap your hands loud enough to startle the couple sitting at the next table. They look at the both of you briefly, then return to their business.

'All the patients hit the floor,' you say, 'but I'm the only son of a bitch standing. Except for the counselor. There they were, cupping their hands over their ears.'

'That was funny?' she asks.

'I'm going to keep doing it for the hell of it—'

'You still attend?'

'If I ever get caught for dealing,' you say, 'I can plead insanity. Blame it on the war.'

'They know you sell drugs for a living?'

'Sure, but they don't care. Those guys have tried everything. Even suicide.'

Carla fidgets with her purse, looks for something within it, but doesn't find it.

'Everybody there's fucked up.'

The waitress comes over to find out if you want anything else. You tell her you're fine for now, but that in a while you might need another round.

'Speaking of another round,' Carla suggests, looking at your shirt pocket.

'Not hooked?' you say.

'We can go to the beach later,' she says.

'When we wake up.' You take a drag of your cigarette.

'I've got nothing to do tomorrow,' she says.

'Correction, today.'

'We've got nothing to do today.'

'Bacardi awaits at home,' you say, fishing for the plastic bag in your pockets.

'I promise I won't do it all,' she says.

You give her the bag. She takes it to the bathroom again, where she stays for a long time. You wonder if she's sharing it with some of the other women in the stalls.

Alone again, you watch how the band keeps the rhythm up by dancing while they play their instruments. Glitter sparks off their billowing shirt sleeves. The couples around you have left their tables for the dance floor.

Carla is all you can think about.

You imagine her inside one of the bathroom stalls, leaning over the toilet, scooping out a tiny mound of the white powder with one of her little flattened spoons or a house key, and snorting it.

Or she might be simply going to the bathroom, looking at the floor cracks.

Like little rivers, you think.

You signal the waitress. She comes over and you order another round. Before she leaves, you drop the hundred dollar bill on her tray and thank her. She looks surprised. For the steady, well-done supplies. Toast to that, she says. A little something to make her night.

She leans close to your ears and says thank you. Her breath smells of peppermint. A faint aroma of papaya shampoo in her hair. Her warm hand on your shoulder, a gentle squeeze.

You watch her dance her way back to the bar.

Nights like this are meant for everything broken: things, people, shards of light across the floor like skin. Your job is to pick them up, dead fingers, ears, one by one, string them around your neck, their sweet scent wafting to your nostrils. It's only a matter of time. This rushing of thoughts about people and places you want to forget. The damaged, hollowed left behind. Nights like this the world should catch fire, burn to the ground, ravage the land in one giant swoop of flame, taking you with it, so you can move on.

Bombardment

WHEN I close my eyes, I see the ropes.

Ropes hanging from the paneled ceiling. Ropes and their round metal necks to signify to the climber this is the limit, as far as you can go. This is a gym in Henry T Gage Junior High School in Los Angeles, California. This is circa 1974.

When I close my eyes I see the braided mesh wire between the glass panes high up on the gym windows where ash and sepia-colored pigeons flock to roost.

When I close my eyes I see the crow, there to steal another pigeon's egg, breaking it open between its own claws, tasting the yolk, looking down at us.

It squawks twice, then takes off with the broken egg in clenched claws.

When I close my eyes I see each letter in the word *bombardment* fall from the rafters down to the bleachers. A bee's buzz around the basketball score-keeper. The 'o' of our mouths when Mr Stupen barks at us to pick teams, knowing how it is going to go.

Lil' Ruben and Ratboy Marcos choose their own team of homeboys—they, of course, are to be shirts, though they sometimes wanted to be skins to show off their Virgen of Guadalupe tattoos on their pectorals, shoulders or arms.

When I close my eyes I hear the 'm' stutter of Benny who always plays on our team, the skins, *los carneritos,* as they call us for *carne,* and he goes down first. Last time he went to the clinic with a bruised rib that hurt like a motherfucker. He believes that once a rib breaks you have less luck in life. Maybe so, Benny. Maybe so.

One time, Chempo, the meanest of them all, got his nose broken. B is for ball. Bad ball. For its heavy, dark weight that bruises the skin where the ball makes contact with our bodies.

A is for the assholes who gang up against us, allow to do so by the lack of supervision by the fucked-up gym teachers. Mr Stupen, bless his masochist heart, never once looked in on us after he blew his whistle to signal the beginning of the 50-minute bout.

'May the last man standing win,' he'd say, turn around, and leave for a smoke or a nap, or, rumor had it, spy on the girls in the locker room through a peep hole in his office.

When I close my eyes I see the 'R' of his striped referee shirt.

Stinky Watson, the only white kid on the team, likes to spit loogies into our faces. He spits them like bullets. After each spit, he works the mouth and tongue, saving up some more saliva.

'M' is for *mierda,* for what I always said when I found two or three of Watson's spits in my hair. Though I never liked to shower at school, I would have to. I hated it the sound Watson made as he hocked up another one.

When I close my eyes I see the entanglements of flesh, how one boy falls on the ground and then there'd be a pile-up. Who didn't believe in the story of Humpty Dumpty, the little egg that fell of the fence and fell apart? You could almost hear the extinction of breath from the victim.

All of us moved back at the start of the game. If there were rules, they were not followed as the homeboys ganged up against us, one by one, drawing us away from the walls to the center of the court where they could take better aim with the bombardment ball and nail us on our backs.

'T' is for the hollow *thuck-thuck* of that ball hitting our flesh.

'Pinches cabrones,' Ramirez, the Mexican, would say. He was made crazy at school by bombardment.

When he and his family crossed the Rio Grande, bombardment wasn't the school activity he had in mind. He said he'd much rather work in the factories, and he did. A year after they broke his arm, he left school. We never heard from or saw Ramirez again. We need you now, Ramirez. Where are you?

There are three Cubans on the skins team and we bonded. We fight back. I stop fighting after they take me down one day and tie me up with the climbing ropes. I believe they will hang me. And if they hang me, I will not ever have to do this again. And they hang me all right, but all they do is line up and throw the ball at my body as hard as they can.

I hang there and they taunt me. A couple miss, and most of the blows come down below the waist. I cover my groin and my head as I try to guess which way the ball is coming at me.

Fifty minutes lasts an eternity. I can hear the sound of my own heart beating between my burning ears. If there is blood coursing through my veins, it is like the Almendares River of my childhood in Cuba gushing after a downpour.

When that bell rings, Mr Stupen never even bothers to come back and blow the whistle, so the gangsters run at us, stampede us with their kicks, wild-thrown punches. They snap their moist-with-sweat, stinky shirts at us.

They claw and tear through our shirts, ripping them off our waists, taking the good ones and keeping them.

Thank God we didn't share lockers with any of them. Us, the recent arrivals from Cuba, Mexico (Tijuana,) Salvador, Nicaragua…we're all wetbacks. Nobody wants us for locker partners. Shit, that's what they call us. The skin shits.

'Wetback skins,' someone shouts and then there are the whistles to signify the bomb-ball's drop.

This is warfare. A ball rains down from the I-beam rafters. The *thuds* of the ball hitting our bodies echoes ad infinitum, loud enough to see the pigeons, sparrows, crows aflutter. They are our only audience. Our only witnesses. I say they are the choir in some Greek drama.

When I close my eyes I see the heavy ball falling from the sky.

'*Wachale!*' someone shouts. 'Take cover!'

In my nightmares there's more than one ball. They rain down upon us, knocking us to the ground, breaking our bones.

Nobody ever speaks about this.

We hide our bruised limbs as best as we could. From our families.

From our parents. 'What's that?' my father will say looking at a bruise on my arm peeking through my t-shirt sleeve. 'Nothing,' I say.

Most of us are twelve, thirteen, fourteen—we don't have to show our bodies to anyone. 'Why are you limping?' my mother wants to know. 'Shoes,' I tell her. 'A little tight.'

The bruises bloom and darken our skins, spilled ink in water, a flowering right underneath our epidermis where the hurt sends shock-waves to our brain, our hearts.

When we close our eyes we see our broken souls.

When we close our eyes we see the scoreboard and how much we are behind, how much we are losing, how much harder we have to try to keep from going down for good.

When we close our eyes we see nothing but the purple and yellow of our cowardice. How, though we keep getting up and dusting our hands off, we keep getting pushed down, ground by a stranger's heel, our cheeks to the hard earth, our ears tuned to the muted sound of some poor sap somewhere moaning about a nosebleed, a broken finger, a fistful of hair missing.

Thuck-thud, thuck-thud, when we close our eyes we can still hear the most frightening of sounds: a bombardment ball rolling across an empty gymnasium court floor, coming to a final rest under put-away bleachers.

We hear ourselves crying, 'Stay close, stay together, stay…."

What is the sound of such a big ball whizzing by you, thrown with deliberate speed, with deliberate maliciousness?

What is the sound of that ball, that ball, hitting your rib cage, knocking the wind out of you? Or hitting the back of your head and knocking you down and out, teeth ground into the wood of the floor?

How does your blood taste as you tilt your head up to keep it from trickling down your mouth and chin? It's blood-in-the-water mentality—one drop and they see your weakness. They'll set upon you and beat you to a pulp.

You don't want to let them know your hurt, your pains and aches, the throbbing between your ears. It's a matter of time, you think. It's only a matter of time before something happens and all this fades away.

Nowhere to run, or hide. Stand up straight. Find out your next move. *Move!*

Now keep your eyes closed to pretend this heavy, scuffed ball is never going to find you.

Jinetera Logic

HER CUSTOMERS called her 'Baby.' Because of her sweet, young face. She was only sixteen now, two years after she arrived in Havana from the province of Pinar del Rio, Cuba. Her roommate Nancy called her 'La Beibi.' Always making fun. She knew her roommate, being six years older than her, was jealous. *Celosa.* Both of them never brought men to this tiny apartment off, off El Vedado, almost all they could afford and still be close to the good hotels like Havana Libre—not that good, but not a dump either, pretty good reputation, and plus the guys who work it know when to look away.

La Beibi, that's her name, and she likes it better with Nancy's pronunciation. Nancy is mulatta, almost six feet. She's lanky because she used to play on the Cuban National volleyball team, until she hurt her knee, then that was it. Until they both became *jineteras,* which in Havana literally meant female jockeys, but also prostitutes.

Everybody had a story in this business. Nancy's story wasn't as bad as hers. If you want to know her real name, you've got to pay extra. If you want to get close enough to her ear to whisper it, then it'll really cost you. Call her 'Baby' and you're fine. That doesn't cost much.

She and Nancy have been together now for almost a year. They know how to live together, and that's simply by staying out of each other's way, and not bringing work home. Not even talk of work. They share a walk-in closet too full of clothes. Hard earned clothes. Dresses of all kinds. Pants. Silk blouses she wishes she'd wear to go back home one day. But she can't. She's made a promise to herself. She'd never go home. If anything she wanted to leave the island. Go someplace else, not necessarily Miami or some other city in the E.E.U.U., as she called the United States. She always laughed when she saw it spelled this way in Spanish-language newspapers. E-E-U-U. When she wanted to make fun of someone she'd call him an E.E.U.U., especially the real rich gringo business men looking for a way to bridge the island with the United States. Cotton and corn seed salesmen, Magazine editors, *como se llaman:* journalists, the media moguls like Ted Turner—him with the wedge between his teeth. She'd never let a man with such a wide gap between his teeth go down on her. Are you crazy? She'd have to shave, and she wasn't about to do that. Nancy did it all the time. Paint her toe nails too.

Nancy shaved designs on hers. *Chocha,* the Cuban boys call it. *Boyo. Crica. Rica crica.* Once she dyed little patches in the Italian flag colors because she said Italian men were the best. They were animals in bed. Nancy was the one who taught her how to do *la espuela,* the spur, on her customers. The finger in the ass right as they were coming, or some liked it all the time, before, during, and after. Some of the tourist bastards really wanted boys, but they went with young girls too, the ones with really short hair, and they loved to do it doggy style, *como los perros.*

Except she hated the spur. If she hated the man, she'd bite her fingernail first, lift a little sliver curlicue edge so that it scratched on the way in. They wouldn't really notice much until they started bleeding, then she wished she could be there, to see the scared expression on their faces. She also wanted to write with lipstick on the bathroom mirrors: *Tu nueva vida con* SIDA, but she didn't want to be turned in to the authorities. If there was anything scarier than the Cuban vice police was a disgruntled male tourist who got offended easily and wanted revenge. She'd heard the stories of other girls being taken out to a field and hacked to death with a machete because someone paid to have it done.

In this island anything goes, she liked to repeat all the time as she put make up on in the mirror. Nancy on the bed with a black scarf around her head to shield her eyes from the light. They had electricity and water longer than most other houses. They were hooked up good, except when there was a citywide blackout, then everyone was in the fucking darkness.

'In this island, *mucho* pussy, Baby,' she'd say and smile, hoping Nancy would wake up and make some coffee. Nancy made the best coffee, syruppy and with a lot of foam. *'La nata,'* Nancy called the whipped up sugar foam.

'That's what happens to the milk,' she'd argue with Nancy.

'La leche,' Nancy would repeat and laugh. Leche was what the fat Spaniards called their semen.

Disgusting, she thought. All men were fucking animals. Sickos. In the two years since she'd been down in Havana doing the *jinetera* thing, she'd seen it all. The men who want the impossible. The ones with the hernias, the surgery scars, the fat deposits on their backs. The ones with hairy knuckles. Lumps on their thighs. Ones with short penises, the fat ones' dicks, and she always thought of the Hindu snake charmers who played the flute to charm the cobras into an easy, hypnotic sway. She didn't know why that made her laugh until she'd start to suck them and their dicks were so far inside them that it was hopeless. Big ones, fourteen and sixteen inchers that wanted to go into her like knives, and she'd say no, no way, to anal penetration. Unless they paid her double. Some did, and tore her up.

That was why Nancy always said she practiced elasticity, did exercises with the smooth handle of one of her brushes. The handle started thin, and grew tapered to a thick knob. *Cada loca con su tema,* her version of her mother's saying.

Both she and Nancy had been waiting for Mr Right. *El Papi.* The one man they could fall in love with so that they could leave the country. Nancy didn't have any mixed feelings about it. She wanted to get out, and quick.

She, on the other hand, didn't want to leave without first sending a message to her mother in Pinar del Rio. She'd been sending her mother money, always feeling guilty for not telling her about what her crazy *novio/marido* had done to her when she had turned twelve. In the tool shed of all places, right where he kept his *latas* of grease, his broken engine parts, his worn car tires. No inner tubes, those he sold on the black market. Right there, she remembered, he forced her to jerk him off, then shoved himself inside her. She hurt for days.

That same day, she packed a few things, and took off for the bus stop. *La parada de la guagua.* Everyone talked about the *guagua* because it was the way out. It was Jonah in the belly of the beast, and the beast was going somewhere, some place, good or bad. *Algun lado.* No note to her mother, nothing. She finally wrote after she'd arrived in Havana, just to let her mother know that she was still alive.

El Nacional was the first place she came to, already dressed from the bus stop. In La Habana Vieja she loved *Ambos Mundos* Hotel, and Santa Isabel, Costal Valencia, a hostel, very nice and a lot of men with families stay there. They come, leave the family, and go hang out at the bars. Schemers all. Both worlds, *ambos mundos*—she liked that. Clean rooms, thick walls. You could scream all you wanted. Or them, rather, when she bit them, those who wanted that kind of stuff done.

Men with hemorrhoids—really too much—with toes and fingers missing. Circumcised. Uncircumcised. The ones with foreskin, she always washed because she hated *la fana,* the white crud these pig men allowed to linger between the folds of their foreskins. Truly disgusting. The first time she found it on a man, she gagged, and almost threw up right there. The man was from Norway or some other Scandinavian country where she guessed men didn't bathe for weeks. That was also true of the Spaniards, with their sweaty underarm musk, and horrible cheese smell on their feet.

She kept telling herself she was sixteen, and she'd seen it all by now. No romance. No illusions. No dreams, other than leaving. She dreamt of leaving all the time, and Nancy, who had learned to recognize that far-away look in her eyes, called it *La mirada el alla.* The over-there look. The other side. Sure, she thought about it all the time.

Nancy kept her going at times with the stories about all the girls she knew who'd taken off, were in Arizona, or California. Those were like the Cuban provinces, but bigger, farther. Cities like New Orleans (that's where Nancy said she'd love to live) and San Francisco. *Nueva York.* Los Angeles where Hollywood was. All the glamour and movie starts. Andy Garcia, her idol, who was Cuban too, like her. Antonio Banderas—that Spaniard she'd fuck in a heartbeat. Wow, *que hombre.* Actually his style was totally Italian, nothing like the Spanish men she'd been with.

Men with *lunares,* birthmarks, she inspected carefully to make sure that it wasn't Kaposi's Sarcoma, SIDA guys. Those she made them wear condoms. She bought them by the box in the black market. Better to be safe than sorry, another one of her mother's sayings she remembered. *'Es mejor prevenir que lamentar.'*

Men with bad hearts. Bad teeth. Bad hair. No hair. Huge balls. She'd seen them all.

One day soon she'd get out, once she found her way-out man. The one who's willing to take care of her, though she knows she doesn't need a man to do that, but it'd be easier. Sometimes when she thinks about Nancy, and Nancy's friendship, she doesn't know if she would have made it this far.

For the men who don't know why this goes on in Cuba, or the men who know but play innocent, she explains her condition but only after she's made them pay and pay and pay. *Mucho dinero,* honey. What else was there to do, she'd heard herself say countless times before. Why work in a profession? Why work? Period. If there's nothing to buy, nothing to do. How much worthless can Cuban money be?

But this, she reminded herself, always in the old and new transactions, had nothing to do with politics and all to do with money. Everything to do with the oldest tradeoff in the world. Her skin for money. Her looks for money. Her mouth, her lips, her breasts, her buttocks. All of her was for sale, but for a price. *Chocha rica.* Rich.

Nancy called it the code of *etiqueta,* a play on clothing tag and etiquette, the way proper people behave. That was another joke that got her in a good mood.

Here she was in El Vedado, her own place, La Baby, the sixteen year old from Pinar del Rio, money stashed away in a shoe box in the back of the closet. Waiting to get out. It was a matter of time, she could feel it. Maybe not today, or tomorrow, but soon.

Some nights when the sky broke open over the whole city and it rained for three days, her and Nancy slept and rested. She dreamed of the man who'd finally take her out of the country. The way he looked. What clothes he wore. The way he combed his hair. The scent on him. Soft hands. Manicured hands. The hands of a man who didn't work as a carpenter or a plummer. A professional man.

Her *galan* in shining armor, Nancy always said. Nancy was learning English because she wanted to live in New Orleans. She said her dream would come true pretty soon too. She kept her hopes high. She'd been in Habana all her life, and she knew better because she'd been to the outside. She knew what it was like.

At night when it rained the frogs came out and started their racket. And she hated frogs because they reminded her of her lost childhood in Pinar del Rio. She hated them because they hid in toolsheds, in crevices, in the cool shadows. She couldn't sleep until they hushed their mockery.

The rain reminded her of water, and water took her far to other places. One time she almost thought of leaving on a raft, but she knew better—she knew what the sun and sea salt could do to the skin. But she would leave one day soon. Of that much she was certain.

And then she'd start from scratch. Anew. In a place where nobody would know who she'd been. A proper place where she could finally mouth her own name, let others voice her true, god-given name.

Grease

Alvaro's garage stank of car fumes, or spilled gasoline, which made me dizzy ever since I was a kid in Cuba and one of my father's friends visited on his Indian motorcycle. I remember it well, how he kick-started it with a belch of blue-cloud of smoke.

At Alvaro's garage all of my father's friends gathered in the late afternoon, after they all drove there from their factory jobs. I walked there from the high school on Miles Avenue. The garage stood at the corner of Sepulveda and Gage, right across from a Winchel's Donut Shop where, if I had some money left over from lunch, I'd buy a glazed donut or apple fritter. Most of the time, I simply stayed there instead of hanging out waiting for my father to show up at Alvaro's.

Sometimes while I waited—if I didn't wait for my father there, he'd get upset—I sat by the pop machine and did homework. Most of the time I watched the men work. Their stained uniforms and boots were the color of crow's feathers. They walked up and down the lanes, between the cars, a silver wink of wrenches in their back pockets. Eladio, Bruno, and Cheo were always talking loud about 'look at this' and 'look at that,' never enough to rouse my interest.

All exiles, these men. They arrived from Cuba and came all the way here to Los Angeles. Most said they came to California for the work.

Alvaro's son, Alvarito, made me look up from reading because he was always calling me names, flicking gobs of grease my way, and I kept ducking them. A couple of times he got me and I didn't find out until I got home and it was too late.

'Pedito,' he'd called out to me, 'Pedote.' I hated it when he called me a fart, and he knew it.

I wanted to call him Captain Hook because of his short little arm and little white hand with the pudgy fingers, but I always held back because he was bigger than me and he had those screwdrivers and hammers at arm's reach. He wasn't that tall, maybe five seven, and I was getting to be five six, so I always thought I could take him, but the one arm on him looked strong. The biceps of his good arm looked pumped, and he'd put the little red devil tattoo on it as if to draw attention away from his little arm and hand.

I asked my father about Alvaro's son one day.

'What about him?' my father said and wiped his forehead with the back of his hand because he too would hear it from my mother if he got grease on his shirt.

'His arm,' I said. 'How did it happen?'

'Ask you mother,' he said and turned the radio on. 'She knows the name of the medicine the mother took.'

I sank in the hot leather of my father's Dodge Dart, a bit confused. Why should I ask my mother? Why would she know?

My father bought this car when we first arrived in Los Angeles from Miami and Cuba before that. He bought it for $500 and my mother hated the car because she said it wasted too much money in gas, and my father kept taking it to fix this or that at Alvaro's garage. I think the honest truth was that she hated for my father to go to that shop. All Cuban men who were up to no good, she always told my father. All that talk about exile, what they lost, what they were back home, what they had. She didn't want to hear any of it. She was tired of the stories. But my father didn't listen, and he claimed that the shop was the perfect place to pick me up because it was between the school and the factory where he worked as a pattern cutter.

One day when I finally asked my mother about Alvaro's son's arm and hand, she didn't know what I was talking about. She kept asking me to describe it.

'I don't know,' I said, 'it looks like a little hand stuck to a little arm.'

She paged through the telephone directory, looking for the address of a meat market she'd heard about. 'Sí,' she kept saying, 'y que más?'

I described Alvarito's hand as best as I could. I even made an analogy to his thick fingers looking like the little plantains my father brought home, these sweet tiny plantains. Like the ones in Cuba.

'Apa said I could ask you, and that you'd know.'

'How should I know? It sounds like he was born like that.'

'Some medicine, my father mentioned.'

She stopped paging through the book and looked up at me. 'Oh, *ya se,*' she said and put her finger to her lips to wet its tip again to turn the pages easier. '*Talidomina.*'

'T-A-L-I-D-O-M-I-N-A,' she spelled it out in Spanish.

I asked what it was in English and she shrugged. 'Ask one of your teachers.'

I thought about the next time Alvarito was mean to me, I might just say the name of the medicine to him. See if that got him to lay off me.

And one day, while I waited at the garage, he kept harassing me about being a sissy, how I chose to play tennis at school instead of football or baseball, and how I kept reading my magazines and books. What was I anyway? Some kind of fairy? He said the word 'fairy' but it sounded like 'furry.'

Alvarito had dropped out of high school and his father made him work in the garage to cover his expenses, in particular the fixing up of a convertible mustang he bought from a junk yard and was working on it piece by piece. With the one good hand, I thought.

So I asked him, point blank, if he knew what Talidomina was. He stopped in front of me, dirty sweat already on his tanned face, a couple of scratches and bumps on his cheeks. He looked at me with his coal-colored eyes, confused, almost absent-mindedly wiping the porcelain of a spark plug.

'What the hell is that?' he asked.

'You know,' I said, 'the medicine.'

'What medicine?'

I swallowed wrong and started to cough. If he didn't know, well…maybe I was pronouncing it wrong and maybe he only knew the pronunciation in English and I didn't know what it was, in English.

'Look,' he said, 'are you sitting there thinking of something to say about my fucking arm?' He stopped and looked underneath a couple of the cars in the shop, as though he had dropped something.

'I can kick your ass with both of my arms tied behind my back, punk,' he said and showed me his yellowed teeth.

I had never been scared of him before then, and suddenly I felt respect. They way he snarled at me like I've seen dogs do to mail carriers. All yellow teeth, saliva froth.

'I've heard it all,' he said, and spat in front of my shoes. 'All the shitty jokes, all my life.'

I sat there sinking. Both feet flat on the ground. My hands moist against my pants.

'Thalidomide,' he said it, pronouncing it in English. 'It's the luck of the cards. My mother took the fucking thing because a doctor prescribed it. There, see? And because she couldn't handle morning-fucking-sickness. . . .'

I didn't know what morning sickness was and why anyone needed to take medicine for it. I felt dumb for not knowing. Suddenly, too, Alvarito looked vulnerable, pained.

'ALVARITO!' someone called from the other side of the shop.

'Coming,' he said and reached over and I thought he was going to knock me out, but he merely tussled my hair. 'It could have happened to you,' he said and walked away.

I sat on that metal chair and felt hot, sweat beads running down the sides of my chest and back.

When my father showed up to pick me up, I ran to the car and got in. I told him to take me straight home. He did. We drove in silence, though he kept asking me every once in a few miles if I heard that noise. The ticking coming from the left side of the car.

'I don't hear it,' I said.

'I'm going to have to take it back in tomorrow.'

And for days and afternoons to come, I would dread going back to Alvaro's garage, feeling like there was nothing left to say, and Alvarito would eventually stop working for his father, after a big fight, take off in his car, drive to Florida, never to be seen or heard from again. Almost the way I'd leave for graduate school, except I kept in touch with my parents, though I wanted not to live with them, their sad small lives.

That afternoon after we arrived home from Alvaro's garage, my parents got into an argument about the car repairs, how much money, all the unnecessary work my father was having Alvaro do. I couldn't concentrate, their voices rising in waves beyond my bedroom door.

After dinner, I went to bed early, turned off all the lights. Closed my eyes to the shadows of the tree branches planted outside my window. I thought of Alvarito's arm, thick and short. I thought of his pinked and grease-smudged fat fingers. The tiny nails with the dirt and grime underneath each of them. His little pinky hardly possessed any nail at all.

I thought of hands like that, wrapping around my neck, even in their smallness. Gripping, tightening, choking the breath out of me. Smothering my life out the way mechanics stub out cigarettes under a heavy, oil-smeared boots.

Corners

RAUL stands on the curb as his boss's green van turns the corner. Good riddance, Raul thinks, what an asshole. Ortega, his father's friend who gave him this job for the summer, is a tightwad, and that van of his is a rolling disaster. Any morning now it's going to fall apart over the railroad tracks. Raul can see those front wheels spinning off their drums, rolling down the street, and the van grinding its nose into asphalt, a beached green whale. This thought makes him smile as Raul bends over and picks up the wire scraper, brushes, and the can of brick-red paint he needs to start on the day's work.

He hates this line of work. Actually, no, he hates all work. He'd much rather be playing ball at the park, but that already got him in trouble. Not only with his parents, sure, but with the police. The cops came to the park to harass him and his friends. Because, the cops said, someone complained about their loitering. What's a park for? he asked the body-building cop, knowing all along he was showing off in front of his friends. The cop didn't appreciate his smart-alecky ass, so he cuffed him and took him in, and because Raul wouldn't shut up in the back, the cop, when they arrived at the station and parked, grabbed him by the hair and pulled him out of the back. It hurt like a mother.

Of course his parents got called in, and now, now he's here practically working free for Ortega, the fat, greasy bastard.

'*Que piensas tu?*' his father asked driving back home from the police station. 'Do you think this kind of behavior is okay?'

Raul sat in the back seat and looked at the backs of his parents head. His mother nodding each time his father spoke. His father only spoke in questions. Questions for which Raul had grown tired of predictable answers. '*La vida* is going to teach you some tough lessons,' his mother told him.

RAUL STANDS there on the sidewalk by the dying walnut tree and looks at the apartment building in this part of Long Beach called Little Cambodia. He can't believe it, his rotten luck. Shit, shit, shit, he curses and moves closer.

The duplex, one of the many properties Ortega owns in Little Cambodia, is run down, all the window woodwork rotting, making the facade look droopy, like in the cartoons. Stained, raggedy curtains hung behind the cracked glass. The grass grows back in clumps among the patches of weed. The stucco cracks run like rivers up and down the sides. Sparrows have built bushy nests from every other roof tile hole, and which Ortega expects him to empty. Raul can see it now, he'll be up there pulling those nests out, the eggs or chicks falling thirty feet to the ground.

Raul must first do all the prep work on the wood, mostly rotted, termite-infested. Scrape, prime, and paint the porch. It's a lot of fucking work, he thinks, three bucks an hour, bring your own lunch, one break. It's not fair, he wants to say, but his parents warned him if he didn't do this, off he went to Miami to live with his Nazi uncle who promised to 'shape' Raul. His uncle owns a shipyard on the Miami river, and he often tells Raul's father, his brother, to send Raul down. Yeah, send the boy down, we'll put him to weld underwater. Sure. Who needs it.

The way Raul sees it, he'll finish this bullshit job all summer, then finish high school and then hit the road. Go where he wants to go. Hell, he might even go to college, if one takes him somewhere. He'd like to play soccer somewhere, if someone is willing to give him a try out. Hell, the way he sees it he's only sixteen. It's only a matter of time before someone notices him. He wants to go far. Very far. Only he's stuck here for the time being. It's the waiting around he hates. The going nowhere. No use to daydream if you've got to concentrate on painting and scraping, the stuff any fool could do.

MORNING and already the sun breaks through, strong and hot. Raul wipes the sweat off his brow and tips the visor of his baseball cap down to keep the glare out of his eyes. Ortega's due to swing by at noon to check up on him, make sure he's still at work. The shade under one of these eucalyptus trees by the side sure looks good. He could simply lay down and nap, but he doesn't want to get his parents riled up again. He's caught, he thinks, caught like fucking tuna in a net. He's seen them on television.

During the week he's been working for Ortega, Raul has become a good fix-it-all, handy man, that is when he wants to, when he tries, when he gets going on thinking about the possibilities of where he'll go play ball. His mother, also under Ortega's employ at his clothing factory, demanded that Raul do a good job for Ortega, or else. It is the 'else' Raul likes to ponder.

His parents even grounded him for a month. No driving. No friends over. No soccer. This was serious fucking business, his parents said. His father called him a couple of cuss words in Spanish. Raul still thinks about them: *comemierda, estupido.* He translates them into English: shit-eater, stupid. First time he's father ever called him this, though he'd heard his father call other people that. What could he do? Raul feels like things aren't going to work out for him. He fears getting stuck, stranded in the same life he sees his parents have. Work, work, work. Get up early. Go to work. Come home tired. Go to bed early because they have to go to work. 'Bullshit,' Raul mutters. Work is for losers. The only thing he wants to work hard at is his sport.

LITTLE CAMBODIA is no different than where he comes from, Raul thinks. Almost the same worn, tired look to everything. The trees. Buildings. Potted plants. The old folk coming and going. Why is it that the old get that curve on their backs? Who invented the undershirt old immigrant men wear? In this heat, amazing, he thinks. The women with their basset hound sadness to their eyes. Those dark sunglasses that wrap around their heads and makes them look like aliens.

The loud voices of kids playing in a vacant lot across the street rise behind him. Scattered trash clutters the lot. The kids use an old sofa as if it were a pirate's ship. Always kids in the neighborhood. Except here it's the Vietnamese children. Over in his neighborhood are the Mexican kids, the Nicaraguan kids, Cubans like him and his parents. The Cuban old men playing dominos and drinking rum, at Christmas time roasting the pigs in old, cut-open oil drums. They make such a big deal about those pigs. His father's friends, Ortega is one, come over and talk loud, get pretty obnoxious, talking about the old country, life here in the United States where everything is work, work, work. Oh, and all the advice, somebody or other is always putting hand over Raul's shoulder to give him advice: on girlfriends, on school, on cars, on life. The best one comes from his own father: 'Don't cut corners or you turn twice.'

He doesn't get it, any of them, all this advice in Spanish. When he translates them into English, they don't make any sense. They become noise in his ears.

Behind the lot, endless clotheslines from which multicolored clothes hang blocks the view of the tenements. For a moment Raul thinks he knows what kind of people live there. He's been here many times. This is the way in probably looks in the old country. This clutter of life on the move. Getting nowhere. But he is, he thinks, he plans to. Get somewhere. Hopefully far.

According to Ortega, this neighborhood's made up of Cambodians, Mexicans, and Americans who refuse to move away. The Cambodians who live in the duplex are never late paying rent.

While he scrapes the loose flakes, Cambodian children peek out of the front window by the side of the porch. The tallest one, his short hair cropped unevenly over his large, curious eyes, smiles at Raul. A sort of peek-a-boo. At first it's funny, but then the kid keeps doing it, so it begins to grate on his mood. An hour later, the kid is still looking at him with his almond-colored eyes, his short spiky hair, his nose with the pinched nostrils, the birthmark splotched on his neck.

Raul works away at removing the old paint off, brushing as hard as he could to get it all off. Years, he thinks, it's been here, each time the new layer covering the old. And every time he looks up the kid is there looking out at him paint. Raul feels like painting the glass so the kid can't look at him anymore. Spooky little shit.

Raul remembers in history class the teacher showing them a documentary about the Vietnam war and each time the scene with the naked girl running, behind her black clouds of a firebombed village, and the soldier who shoots the man on the head, point-blank, the girls in the class going 'turn it off, turn it off,' and one of the guys saying 'shit-out-of-luck.'

Gross. Sickening. The teacher made them shut up and pay attention, himself a veteran now teaching them in Los Angeles, the 'freshly-arrived' as the teacher called them. 'We keep getting the world out of trouble,' Mr Salvatore said, 'and the world expects it from us. Bad decisions on our part. Vietnam costs us more than we are able willing to pay again. Fifty-thousand casualty. Many more lost every day to drugs. Madness. Suicide....'

Mr Salvatore would get so upset sometimes that he'd have to walk outside the classroom and get some fresh air. Raul would run to the bungalow window and check him out, make sure the coast was safe so that he could rewind the video and freeze it on the naked girl, the guys pointing to her crotch.

THE PAINT, as Raul brushes it in quick, even strokes, covers the stairs smoothly—no need for a second coat, he thinks. He sops it on thick. No way he's coming back another day to do this. If he could have it his way, he'd take off. Teach his parents a lesson. Maybe hit the road, leave for good.

When these feelings of being stuck invade him, Raul cringes, bites down on his lip simply to control rage welling up inside him. He fears not being able to stay in control.

Suddenly the front door opens and the tall Cambodian kid appears.

'Me and my brothers go play,' the kid says.

'Use the back door,' Raul says.

'Back door parents lock.'

Fresh paint covers the steps between the kid and Raul. The kid stands there, his knobby knees almost touching, his thin long toes looking dirty and weird.

'You'll have to wait, okay?' Raul says.

'You pick me up,' the kid says.

'Can't reach you from here.'

'I play now!'

The little monster, Raul thinks, and says, 'When the paint dries, okay?' Give him a break. Raul remembers Mr Salvatore's talk about one culture dumping on another. It's the history of civilization. It's the history of the United States. The dominant culture taking advantage of the weak.

'I tell my grandmother,' he says and closes the door.

A group of kids run across the street screaming like Indians on the attack. Girls stand by the side fence, giggling, pointing to the group of boys on the torn sofa.

If he could only be at the park now, Raul thinks, playing soccer with his friends. What I am doing here? He thinks.

Above him the hungry sparrow chicks cry for their parents to bring them food, and each time Raul looks up, he can't see them. He wishes he could, but that would mean he'd have to carry the ladder over and set it up. Their cries are constant. No parents in sight.

Almost like these kids. Where are the parents? The kids are out running around, and at the sidewalks for when the ice cream trucks come by. Raul hates ice cream trucks. They are big rip offs.

When he finishes the first handrail, he moves the paint and brushes to begin on the other.

The kids behind the finger-print-smudged glass stick their tongues out at Raul as he steps back for a look at what he's accomplished. Not even paint can help, he's decided, so why keep trying.

Raul grins up at them.

The door opens again and this time an old Cambodian woman with the wrinkles of a bed sheet fresh on her face stands there, arms akimbo.

'It's wet,' Raul tells her.

She looks down at the paint. Her pants come up halfway between her knees and her ankles. She too has ugly feet, her toes curving outward because of these great bunions. She's missing a toe on her left foot.

'Understand?' he says, dipping the paint brush into the can. 'It's wet. Wet.'

The woman says something in Cambodian to the kid behind her.

'What you doing?' the kid asks.

'Tell her Ortega told me to paint the porch,' Raul says. The boss man. The owner of the apartments.

The kid speaks to his grandmother who then pushes her grandson back inside and closes the door.

One day he's going to make sure he doesn't own property, rundown shitholes like this one, Raul thinks, and he's not going to let big families live in the apartments he will never own. He can't see himself as the owner of anything. Well, maybe a car. His own house in which to live. Sure, that he could handle.

But no kids. Too many kids get out of hand; they ruin everything.

A few strokes short of finishing, the tall kid runs out of the apartment, stepping on the paint. His little footprints on the still-wet paint. Raul cannot believe it. The kid has balls.

Raul chases after the kid, catches up, and picks him up by the waist.

'Let go!' the kid says, banging on Raul's back. 'Let go, you!'

'Little bastard,' Raul yells. 'Didn't I tell you to wait until the paint dries, huh?'

Raul carries the kid back to the apartment where the grandmother waits.

'Keep his ass inside,' Raul tells her. He tries to let her know with one look how angry he is. Can't they see he doesn't want to be here? He's not coming back to paint all this again, no way.

She yanks the kid back inside and shuts the door. The blackened doorknob rattles when she slams the door.

Ortega'll be here soon, Raul thinks, trying to find a way to cover up the footmarks. This, he guesses, is the kind of shit he'll have to put up with for the rest of the summer. Here, in the other properties, everywhere he goes to paint.

When he talks to his friends at school, they make fun of him because he's trying too hard to fit in. He wants to blend, melt, whatever it is they call it in history class. This melting pot big deal. How people come to the United States and take part in American daily life. How they enter the mainstream, begin to lose their old culture. Raul doesn't care about that. He wants to be left alone to do what he likes to do. He's lived in this country longer than anywhere else. He doesn't even remember Cuba, the place his birth. His parents sure do remember it. Always talk to him about it. But he lives here now. This is where he's going to make it.

ALL THE PAINT in the world couldn't begin to hide all the shit, crap, of the world. He straightens and laughs at his own thought. He images those brush fire helicopters carrying instead of buckets of water, buckets of paint, drizzling paint on every city in Los Angeles county, over everything, houses, trees, cars, people. People will come out of their houses to go to work or school and Splash! Get painted. Ruined dresses. New suits. Work clothes. And he'd paint everything an ugly, bright purple, or maybe blue. He likes the possibilities of blue.

He can almost hear his father on the phone, to complain to the authorities that his son has gone crazy painting everything in the neighborhood blue.

ONCE HE FINISHES covering up the marks, Raul walks to the nearest tree and sits in the shade to wait for the van. Ortega will soon arrive to pick him up, take him to another in-need of paint place.

How can he give up? Raul thinks, on his summer. This one summer in his sixteenth year. No way, man. But everything points in the direction of wasted. Going up in the heat of this day.

Suddenly the front door flings open. Raul bolts up into a sitting position. He can't believe it.

The kid runs outside again, this time his brothers and sisters follow.

Their grandmother watches as they cross the street. A car almost hits the last one who is completely naked.

Raul stands, approaches the woman, and says, 'Why did you let them out?'

The woman leans against the door frame with a look of satisfaction widening her gray eyes.

'Lady,' he says raising his voice, 'I'm trying to get this job done.' He's going to tell Ortega to evict their asses out of here, he wants to say, but doesn't it. He holds the words in and they choke him, they become bricks in his throat, hard and unpalatable.

All the paint's gone, so Raul has to get water out of the faucet by the side of the house and thin some of the paint at the bottom of the can. No matter how many times he runs the brush over the stairs, the footprints remain. 'The little son of a bitch,' Raul says under his breath. He should kick his Cambodian ass.

Ortega's green van is due to turn at the corner any minute now.

Pushing the other kids off the sofa, the Cambodian kid jumps up and down, kicks up clouds of dust around their feet and legs. They are shouting something in Cambodian to Raul. He knows they are mocking him, making fun of him for all the times he's fucked up. For all the times he's held back. For all his failures.

Raul bends over the stairs and tries frantically to cover the marks. The oldest kid pounds on his chest like some great gorilla and howls from the top of his lungs. Raul feels like none of this is part of what he came here to do. Suddenly, sadness fills him like this coat of thin paint he's laid down. Not enough color to cover the old, the worn, the utterly ugly. Like so much of his life, he thinks. He's beginning to think that around the corner, there's no way out. Nowhere to go. Dead ends everywhere.

The Vietnamese children mock him. They point at him an accusatory finger as though to say: *you, you're not one of us, you don't belong here.*

Their howls are loud enough to get the sparrow chicks crying all over again.

Armadillos

THEY COME through in the night.

He hears them outside the window, nuzzling under dead leaves, scratching the ground for worms, tasty morsels. They nose around, dig down to the fattest grubs. Armadillos, he's convinced, are not of this world, with their armor, the way their tiny ears angle up like silver radar dishes.

How do they do it, find their way in the night? One minute evading the heat of day in their burrows, the next scavenging lawns by starlight. Destroying them. Pock-marking them. Rooting through azaleas, prize daisies.

Armadillos, the great insomniacs of the animal kingdom, that's why you find them flattened on country roads, squashed by trucks in the middle of cool nights. Cracked armor, festering coils of entrails and sinew. Crows love them. Hawks too. Up, sleepless, hungry, then dead by the roadside.

Rich sleeps, having stayed up for two nights—it's their fault, he wants to say, that he sleeps so poorly—they wreck his lawn, his pride and joy. It's taken him several months to get the St Augustine grass growing neat around the walks and flower beds.

When he bought his house, no others were going up. The realtor assured him his would be the only one here on Journey's End, that the lots surrounding his property wouldn't be developed for at least ten years. Yet this summer, builders started on the empty lot next to his house. All that space available, and they chose to build another house right up against his. Construction's what has set the armadillos running. Scared the armadillos out of their burrows, all that cutting-down of trees, moving of earth. There must have been a nest of them somewhere.

Rich knows armadillos aren't stupid, which is why he's declared war on them. He's declared it on his soon-to-be-moved-in neighbors, too. In the night, when he cannot sleep, he walks over and removes nails, dismantles 2×4s with his own saw. A couple of cuts in the right places and the frame comes down. He's done this a few nights until he realized that it was a losing battle, as much as he'd like to stall the construction, the builders just keep fixing it, doing more each day. It's inevitable.

For weeks the sound of the house next door going up ruined his concentration. He'd gotten a new job here in Bradenton teaching composition to undergraduates at a nearby little college, a go-nowhere job but he wanted to be closer to his mother. His father'd passed away during the recovery period after colon surgery. The Friday he was supposed to be discharged to go home, a massive coronary laid him low.

The ICU Code Blue surgeon blamed it on a blood clot. 'These things happen,' he explained, pulling the vermillion mask from his mouth. These things *do* happen. Rich remembers his students' excuses over the years, drunken uncles killed in car crashes, grandmothers who tumbled down staircases, knife fights, drunken brawls with loaded guns, tractor trailer explosions on the highway … *these things happen.*

Like the damn armadillos coming through and tearing up his lawn. He wants not to think about them, or cancer, or all the craziness that keeps him awake at night.

He moved back to Bradenton because it was a quiet, no-nonsense place where he could work on his book of comparative paragraph structures in student compositions. But since he's come back he hasn't touched the manuscript. His father's dying sort of settled things for him. What's the hurry? It wasn't like he was up for tenure. Heck, nobody really bothered much with him. He likes his invisibility in the department. It's his habit to only show up when he needs to. He prefers to teach his classes, be good to his students, and rush back home.

Other than checking up on his mother, taking her to buy the groceries at the Publix, watching football games, he sits on his chair on the porch and shoots at the armadillos. There are nights when he thinks he is winning the war, but then he wakes up in the morning and finds his lawn pockmarked with more holes.

During the summer nights, the insects fly up from the tall grass to the street floodlights. They flit and flash against his windows. The frogs gorge themselves on moths and mosquitoes, these green tree frogs that speck his window screens, their translucent bellies flattened against the wire mesh.

He hoses bug spray onto his forearms and legs, wears his jeans and a t-shirt, brings out a six-pack cooler of Rolling Rock and drinks outside through the night. Drinks and ponders his days as a teenager. He played baseball in high school, but then he hurt his arm pitching. Afterwards, a lot of his buddies stopped calling, hanging out. Rich didn't really date much back in those days, and in college he spent too much time at the library. Now, he's afraid he'd violate fraternization rules, sexual harassment laws, so he leaves his door wide open during teacher-student conferences. He cringes when the young girls call him 'sir' or 'professor.'

Not much has happened in Bradenton in the past twenty years, and not much will in the next twenty. He likes it like that. His parents loved it too, that's why his father, the office furniture, chose to relocate to this spot on the Gulf coast when Rich was three. They always nodded when they talked about Bradenton being the right choice. His father was a soft-spoken man who liked a good joke, and a good round of cheap golf too.

Rich remembers his father shooting at the armadillos to dissuade them from rooting into his tomato garden. It's been a long, long fight, Rich thinks while he drinks more beer and reloads. Once, Rich shot a possum because the animal startled him with its ugly snout, and sharp claws right there on the porch. He simply pulled the trigger and the animal fell onto its side and stopped breathing immediately.

He buried it beyond the woodpile in his backyard.

That'd been many nights ago, perhaps a year or two ago. That's also what he appreciates about Bradenton, that time passes unabashedly. *He's in the right place.* Rick sits there, watching it ease from darkness to dawn, a bleaching of the night sky he loves to see.

Tonight he spots a female scuttling from around a pine. She's with a couple of babies, trailing not far behind. The babies stop to sniff the air.

Rich takes a swig of his beer, feeling it cool his throat. Then he takes the rifle, aims at one of the babies, then changes his mind and targets the mother. *Mother 'll have more babies,* he thinks.

He pulls the trigger. The report startles the babies. Rich reloads and aims at the bigger of the two babies, but it's too late. They scram across the street and into the tall grass.

Rich walks over to the dead armadillo, kicks its armor, and studies the damage. Clean off. No head.

He picks up the animal by the tail, carries it over to where the babies headed, and swings the mother's corpse into the darkness. That'll teach them, he hopes. In a few days they'll be back, Rich knows, but for now it'll get him a few days of peace. Maybe.

When morning comes, he surveys the yard in front and around the house, throws the beer empties in the green recycling bin, folds the chair and goes inside to sleep. He teaches mid-afternoon and early evening classes on Tuesdays and Thursdays. He is always home.

He steps inside, removes his shoes and leaves them by the door, then steps on the plush carpet of the living room, places the chair behind the door, drops his father's rifle, now his Armadillo eradicator, on the couch and goes to the bedroom to sleep.

Tonight an indigo 1970 Nova with the mag tires and hood flair paint cuts its lights and drives up on the neighbor's driveway. Rich has been on armadillo vigil for a few hours. He's taken out a half dozen beers already. Despite the bug spray, the mosquitoes are biting and it's hot, muggy.

He didn't see the car come around the corner at first, but he turns toward it when it cuts its lights and crunches up the gravel of the driveway next door. Luckily Rich knows he'd never be seen because he sits in the porch with the lights off, though the streetlight floods the entire corner lot and part of the neighbor's. He sees perfectly from where he lurks.

The car with its dark, shiny hood and top, idles there, moonlight glinting off its slick paint.

Muffled music comes from inside the Nova. It sounds like 'Brass in Pocket' by The Pretenders, or some other 80s band.

In high school he'd had a buddy with a Chevy Nova like this, only a lot less nice. They cruised up and down the main drag, still too young to sneak into the bars, and besides the college girls made fun of them because they were still a couple of dumb teenagers who looked it.

The driver shuts the engine and soon enough its sound is replaced by those of the night. Crickets, frogs, insects tick against things.

Someone inside changes the stations.

Rich hears music again, more scanning, hesitation, and then a song he swears he recognizes but not really because it'd been a long time since he's listened to the radio. He enjoys television better, and only when it's a necessity. He watches football, and every once in a while a movie on HBO.

From where Rich sits, he can see how the driver, a young man, rolls down his window and lights a cigarette. The illumination of his face and long, blond hair in the match's brief flash.

'That's cool,' the young man says.

'…Damn it!…'

'Leave it, leave it.'

The young man smokes. He takes a long puff, holds it for a long time, then exhales. Rich sees smoke plume out of the car window and rise in the light.

'How you get this thing off?'

Rich makes out a young woman's voice. It's a bit drawn, raspy, of someone who's been drinking. Slurred words, feebly chosen.

There is quiet, then Rich observes the car moving. He imagines some hanky panky going on. The two bodies move from the front seats to the back. Then come knocks and thumps.

The thought of what those two are doing hardens in the back of Rich's mind and stays there, like the gulp of warm beer he retains in his throat, feeling the suds dissipate. He swallows and makes up his mind.

He rises from his chair quietly, puts the beer down and then as he takes his first step, he knocks the bottle over. He freezes.

The car keeps rocking in the moonlight.

Rich moves from under his porch and walks toward the pine trees on his front lawn, away from the car, but comes around so that he can see through the rear windows.

As he draws closer, he feels the heat on his back. The light shines bright and for an instant he almost changes his mind. The surprise of what he thinks he is doing keeps his adrenaline up, pulsing down his legs and arms so they become tense, his back stiffens. He holds tightly to the rifle, keeping the barrel facing toward the ground.

What does he think they are doing, those two? Having sex, he thinks. Having sex in a car parked in his neighbor's drive.

As he moves in closer, he sees them, a young man and a young woman, in the back seat, white flesh flashing in the moonlight, between light and shadow. Rich hears them. A belt buckle hitting something. Ash tray? Rich can almost feel their breathing, the boy's voice so low in the girl's ear: 'Oh, man, oh, man. . . .'

Something elastic snaps against flesh, and then everything stops. All sound ceases inside the car.

Rich leans in as much as he can to get a closer look, but he can't see more than a bulk leaned over—two bodies close together.

She mutters something Rich can't make out. What did she say?

A frog starts to croak near the car and Rich doesn't hear it. What he does hear is the sound of his own heart pounding deep inside his chest. He stands still, but continues to look inside the car.

Now he hears a buckle being unclasped, and the car begins to rock again. Rich brings the rifle up and holds it in both hands as he tilts closer toward the back window, close enough to see his own reflection in the glass.

'Amazing,' the young man says, then he slides his partner onto her back and crawls on top of her. Now the car sways, and Rich can't look away. The girl's white legs are up, the bottoms of her feet hitting the ceiling.

Then there's a scratching, a rustling, that same sound that's been haunting his dreams, the same sound that's been in his woodpile, his yard, his house, his mind.

Rich recoils, takes a step back and aims the gun at the bodies tangled in the back seat of the 1970 Nova. He places his finger on the trigger. What drives people to behave like animals? he thinks. They're no better than insects, than rodents, than armadillos. Not these two.

He feels the trigger move beneath his finger.

A man draws a line somewhere. This is his house, his property. This is the place where he just wants a little peace. Who would believe this? he thinks, a grown man peeping on a couple of punks screwing in a car in the middle of the night?

Who would believe his story of a man at war with nature?

Flash Flesh

———

WHEN WE MOVED from Miami to Los Angeles, we lived in an apartment building on Marbrisa Street, across from a McDonald's. One day I was sitting on the front stairs of the building, waiting for Julio, my Nicaraguan friend, to get home so we could play catch. The stairs was my favorite spot for sitting and looking out at the street. Nothing new was happening, just the usual: women sweeping leaves and dust off their porches, men working under the hoods of their cars.

I sat there gripping and shaping the McGregor glove my father had bought for me at Thrifty's. It would take a while to break into the new leather. Then, out of nowhere, it seemed, a *vato* or *pachuco,* as the people who knew them in the neighborhood called them, came walking down the sidewalk, arm-in-arm with his girlfriend.

It was Sunday, so they were sporting their best clothes: he with crisply-creased chinos, a Pendleton shirt buttoned to the collar, a sparkling belt buckle and shiny black shoes; she with a white, low-cut blouse too short to cover her belly button, cords and white sandals.

She also wore so much make up and eye shadow that her face looked like a mask. Her hair stood in a curl over her pale forehead, the rest of it spilling over her brown shoulders and the front of her big breasts. Her corduroy pants were tight, even tighter in the crotch, so tight I thought of my hand in my glove and how the leather stitches welted against my fingers.

The *vato,* seeing me eyeing him and his girlfriend, walked up to the stairs where I sat and said, 'Hey, *ese,* where you from?'

'Cuba,' I said.

'A *Cuba-Cubanito*,' he said and turned to the young woman. 'This is my *ruca*. Say hello.'

'Hello, Ruca,' I said, not knowing that *ruca* meant girlfriend.

'Ruca's not my name,' she said.

'She's *La Gata de la Trece, ese*,' he said, reaching into his shirt pocket, from which he withdrew a pack of Marlboros. 'You want one,' he said and tapped out a cigarette.

'I don't smoke,' I said and placed the glove on the step between my legs.

'Umm,' he said and lit his cigarette. He acted real suave and let the smoke swirl around his face. He blew the rest in front of me.

It was then I noticed the tear tattoo under his right eye and *La Vida Loca* written in script on his neck. 'What you looking at, *ese*?' he said.

'Nothing,' I told him.

'Hey, *pendejo*, how old are you?'

'He's a kid,' she said.

'Twelve.'

'Twelve,' he said and laughed. 'Old enough.'

I should have stood up then and gone upstairs to a world more familiar to me, but I kept staring at the woman's breasts, at the V of her cleavage and the soft skin there.

'You have any money?' he asked.

'No.'

'Can you get some?'

'What for?' That was the wrong question.

'What for? What for?' he said, then. 'Are you insulting my girl, eh?'

'No,' I said.

'If you get a ten,' he said and stopped to put his hand on her breast, 'she'll show you something.'

'Cut it out,' she said, getting his hand away from her breast.

'With, *mira*,' he said and rubbed the tip of his fingers, 'with ten dollars, you can see her *panocha*.'

Panocha. I didn't know what that was, but it was clear that it was to be some part of her anatomy.

I kept hoping someone would come to the rescue, like Julio, but no one did. I was alone on this one.

He started to grab the woman, and she kept fending him off. I didn't know how these two could be together, but something kept my attention. He pawed at her flesh, of which I was seeing some.

In one attempt, he pulled down her blouse and grabbed one of her breasts. 'See this,' he said and smiled. 'You see this mark right here.'

I looked at her flesh. I saw the brown pink of her nipple, then the hickie he pointed to. 'I gave her this,' he said.

I looked on.

'Stop it, *no chingues*,' she said, slipping her breast back inside her blouse.

'Okay, *ese*,' he said. 'You can have her if you give me your glove.'

I told him I couldn't do it, my father would kill me.

'INSULT NUMBER THREE,' he shouted. 'Shit. You keep offending my woman.'

I put my foot on the glove.

'*¡Orale!* Okay,' he said. 'Tell you what, if you give me the glove, she'll let you see her *panocha*.'

He worked furiously at unbuckling her belt, the cigarette dangling from the corner of his mouth, a strand of his slick hair falling over his eyes.

I was speechless. I didn't know whether to run or shout for help. When he couldn't do it, her pants being too tight, he shoved his hand inside her pants and grabbed her crotch. She screamed and started to hit him with her fists. Suddenly he pulled his hand out. He presented his closed hand to me. 'Look here,' he said, opening his fingers one by one.

In between his fingers were curly pubic hairs. He picked them one by one and threw them at my face. '*Pendejos, pendejos, pendejos,*' he said. 'Perfumed pubic hair. How about it, *pinche cabrón?*'

'Let's go, Victor,' she said. 'Leave him alone and let's go.'

'No,' he said. 'Can't you see it in his eyes. He likes you.'

Victor brought his fingers close to my face again. I froze. With one hand on my shoulder, the hand with the cigarette—I feared he would burn my ears—he held my attention and touched the tip of my nose with the fingers of the other hand. He rubbed the smell, her scent, under my nostril, then touched the tip of my nose. I pulled my head back and he let go. He was smiling, and I could see the pink of his tongue behind his dirty teeth.

'Okay, but let's get out of here,' she said.

'No, last deal, my friend,' he said. Once he was done smoking, he flicked the butt on the floor and crushed it out with his shoe. The gutted cigarette on the sidewalk blew away with a gust of wind.

'For your glove,' he said, 'she will pull on your slinky.'

'No, *ya vámonos*,' she said.

'How about it, *Cubanito pendejito?*'

'Gotta go,' I said and stood up.

He tried to grab the glove off my hand but I was quicker than he was. Then, my moving up the stairs with the glove upset him.

'*¡Orale cabrón,*' he said. 'Don't let me catch you around here anymore or I'll kick your ass. If not me, then one of my homeboys.'

I walked up and stopped at the top of the stairs, turned and looked down one more time. He was saying, '. . . insulted my *ruca* and I don't like that. Nobody insults *La Gata de la Trece* and gets away with it.'

I left them both there and hurried to my apartment, opened the door, put the glove down on the sofa and closed the door behind me. My mother was sewing in the bedroom; my father was napping on the easy chair.

I went to the bathroom and stood by the sink. I closed my eyes and thought of the girl and her flesh. The sweet scent of the perfume came up through my nose, a little faint. Flesh. Soft and brown. Her flesh. Pink nipples. The contour of her belly button, the fuzzy hairs there. Her crotch. I looked into the medicine cabinet mirror and saw my own adolescent face. Punk, I thought. I felt embarrassed and humiliated, and yet excited. Extremely excited at the nagging smell rising in through my nostrils.

I was twelve. I thought about how much longer it would be before I became acquainted with the flesh of a woman.

Ricochet

I'M WORKING the rubber band made from a long strip I cut from my bicycle tire's inner tube. The black, powdery residue of the rubber leaves fingerprints on the surface where I'm doing the work. Trying not to get a tear in the rubber. This is the second time I try. I'm hiding in the back yard, by the sink and faucet where my mother usually does the wash, out of reach so nobody sees me, nobody bothers me. I'm thinking I'm going to have the meanest, bestest slingshot musket in the neighborhood. I'm going to shoot lizard's heads off with bottle caps. Fermín, my black friend at school, showed me the original drawing of the thing itself. I copied it and now I'm building it back here by the chicken coops, using my father's hammer, scissors, and a few furniture tacks I removed from the bottom of the sofa. Nobody will miss them, and nobody can see the flap of material hanging loose like a dog's ear.

The rubber holds, dangles around my hands like a pair of black snakes. Fine rubber. The best, which I took from the front wheel of my bicycle. I put the tire back on so my father wouldn't see the thing missing. Only a flat tire, and any bike can have that. I just won't ride it, and if they ask me to I'll say I don't feel like it. My father's been gone for two or three days now. The secret police, as my mother called the two civilian-dressed men, came and arrested my father. I'm here in the house with my grandmother. I haven't seen my parents in a few days.

The G-Dos, secret police, came for my dissident father. My father, the *gusano*—this much I know is true.

Every time I glance over at my bicycle with its flat front tire, leaning against the gate that separates the chickens from the rabbits, I think of my father. He stands in line for days to get me this bicycle, and I know he'll be angry if he ever finds out. My grandmother tells me he'll be back home any minute now, but we haven't heard from him or my mother. The neighbors keep coming by to talk to my grandmother, find out what happened. The next door neighbor, Miriam and her son Chichi, come by and I almost show Chichi my slingshot musket, but then I think better of it. If I show it around everyone will ask questions. They will glance its beauty soon enough.

It's almost done, and I've collected enough bottle caps on the way home from school and back to have a real shoot-out war. Everyone in the neighborhood has slingshots, including Chichi, but nobody has this one. I hold the 2 x 2 piece of wood in my hand, feel its weight on my fingers. I sanded it down on the sides real smooth because I didn't want to get any more splinters in the tips of my fingers. I plan to paint it red or black, like a real pirate's musket I've seen on TV.

My grandmother, who cooks in the kitchen, keeps poking her head out of the kitchen entrance to ask if I need anything. I've been out here for a long time, long enough to get used to the thick, musky smell of the chickens. A rooster hops up to the fence and eyes me the way chickens do. Turns this side first, then the other. I aim the thing at it and pretend I slice its head off. One clean shot. I want to line up the trigger with the front muzzle. I've cut two feet of rubber for each side. I load one side, then the other. Each side holds three bottle cap back-ups, so that I could reload real fast.

Then Ricardito, my friend from the other side of the fence, shows up on top of the fence between his house and mine. I can't hide the musket fast enough.

'What are you doing?' he asks and licks his lips. He always licks his lips when he's nervous.

'Hey, not much.' I want to tell him *not now,* that I don't want to play. But he looks like he isn't going to jump down and leave me alone, so I glare up at him. He's older by two years, but everything we play I always beat him. My mother once told me the story of how when I was three I peed in my bottle and gave Ricardito it to drink from, told him it was delicious orange juice. I don't remember doing it, but my mother says I did.

'Wanna play ball?' he says, his dirty hands gripping the cement at the top of the cinder block wall. His father always threatens to stick broken pieces of bottles up there so we won't jump the fence so often. Ricardito broke his arm once when we used to walk it up and down, balancing ourselves up there like in tightrope acts.

'Not right now.'

'Has your father come back?'

My father, the traitor. My father the counter-revolutionary.

'No, not yet.' I feel the rubber band underneath my thighs as I squat over them so Ricardito won't see them. He's my best friend, but once he sees something of mine he can't stop asking questions.

'My father says they can keep him in prison for good,' he says. I don't want to think about my father, so I don't say anything.

'They'll make him cut sugar cane.' Once you get him going, he can never stop. There's no way to do it unless you get his mind off on something else, I don't because I don't want him to start asking me questions about what I'm doing.

He sits there and dangles his legs over the side. His scuffed shoes scrape against the cement. I can see the worn sole on one shoe, and the crack in the other. He isn't wearing socks and his ankles and calves are riddled with mosquito bites, whole constellations of them, some red, other crusted over with purple scabs. The sores never go away because he loves to pick off the scabs and look at them real close. He told me once he saves them all in a jar, and I believe him. I believe anything he says when it concerns his body.

One time when we were alone in the house, he called me into the bathroom where I had found him with a bloody mouth. He kept spitting up blood and saliva, and when I asked him what had happened he showed me his loose tooth. He'd pulled on a tooth long enough to jiggle it loose, and now his gums were bleeding. This was a permanent tooth too.

Whenever he smiles he's got a gap right there. His parents refuse to take him to the dentist, and his father beat him silly because of it.

'What are you going to do if your father doesn't come back?' Ricardito asked.

'He'll come back.'

'Not if they don't want him to. You think they'll kill him?'

'My grandmother says he'll come back.'

Ricardito hates my grandmother because she always chases him away with a broom. She calls him the little animal, the little pest. *'Animalito,'* she screams at him. *'Salte de aquí! Vete ya!'*

He sticks his big, candy-stained tongue out at her.

Once he fell as he ran and scraped his knees, but he didn't cry. I thought of him that night, in bed, waiting for the blood to dry, crust-up into giant scabs so he could start digging his dirty nails underneath. He says that if you look at the underside of a scab, you could see the patterns of skin as it heals, like when you cut a tree down and count the rings to see how old the tree is. Except his never heal. He bleeds on to his bed sheets, and his mother never asks why, or where the blood comes from. His mother can't see very well. She wears glasses thicker than the bottoms of bottles.

When I realize Ricardito isn't going to go away, I figure I could ask him to get me something. I need a big nail for a trigger. 'Does your father have a nail I can use,' I ask.

'What do you want a nail for?'

'I can't tell you. Does he have one?'

'He might. It depends.'

'If you get me one I will tell you.'

He stares at me with his eyebrows furrowed, like he always does because half of the things I say he never believes, and also because he's too used to my fooling him and pulling his leg all the time. Maybe there's some truth to the bottle of my urine he drank.

No use. I see it in his eyes. He's in one of those lazy moods. I can tell. He doesn't feel like jumping down. What can I do?

'If I tell you what I'm doing,' I tell him, 'do you promise not to tell?'

'I might, might not.'

'*Mierda.*'

He looks hurt because he never likes it when I called him shit. I feel sorry for him all of a sudden.

'All right.'

'Ok,' he says.

'Can't you tell what it is?'

'A slingshot.'

'Better than that.'

'Where did you get the rubber bands?'

I didn't answer, just shrugged.

He jumps down now, his feet landing flat and square by the mound of bottle caps. He lands on it and crushes a few. Startled, the chickens flutter into a ruckus.

'Take it easy,' I say. 'Look where you're jumping.'

He apologizes, but it's no use. I can tell. He wants to know more than ever what it is I'm building.

I show him. 'See, it's a musket, a rifle, a machine gun of bottle caps.'

I explain how I plan to shoot bottle caps at lizards, at birds, at anything I find.

Already he's all hands. I hate that about him, his groping around with his dirty hands and fingernails. He's about to pull on the rubber bands, stretch them for the first time, and I yank them out of his hands.

If I found the nail, and I put the thing together I could convince Ricardito to play firing squad. I heard one of my parents friends mention something about it once. One of my father's friends, Guillermo, who rode the motorcycle—he rode me around a few time, up and down the street, what a great thrill—and he never came home one afternoon. Guillermo was a *gusano,* my parents always called him. *Gusano* means worm, maggot. I found out it means dissident, counter-revolutionary, the kind that could get you killed or disappeared in Cuba. When my father called Guillermo *gusano*, he always shot back: 'It takes one to know one.' And both he and my father laughed real hard.

I can play firing squad with Ricardito, yeah.

We look around the chicken coop and rabbit hutches until I find the right nail, then I pull it out slowly. With one knee on the ground and Ricardito breathing over my head, I straighten it out. It has a wide enough of a head for what I need. The wide head holds the bottle cap under the pressure from the rubber band, and then I can flick it easy like flipping a coin up in the air.

I measure one last time, still making sure that Ricardito doesn't touch any more of the bottle caps—I had them counted—and hammer the nail into place.

'It's done,' I say and hold up my brand new musket. 'Look how beautiful.'

'Can I hold it?' Ricardito licks his dry, cracked lips.

'No yet,' I say and turn away from him until I can load it properly.

The rubber bands stretch just fine, with plenty of tension. I imagine the bottle caps going fast and hard, easily lobbing off the head of any lizard, frog, snake. Great, I think and feel the excitement in my throat.

The rubber band hugs the first three caps, then I load the second one, another three. It's ready.

I want to shoot it before my grandmother hears us.

'Stand against the wall, just straight like that.'

'Why?'

'Just do it,' I tell him.

He backs up against the dirty lime walls in the patio of our house in Habana. A little nervous, he fidgets. His shoulders slump, his hands flutter about in and out of his pockets.

'Move back more, right up against the wall.'

Then I think of the perfect idea. I blind fold him to make it look real enough. Then Ricardito can't see, and he won't know how the thing works, and he'll be too scared to want to shoot it. I figure I could aim for his gut, or his hands.

I find a rag by the sink, take it and fold it over his eyes.

'I can't see,' he says.

'That's the idea.' I turn him a few times like he's going to beat up a *piñata* or pin the tail on the donkey.

Then I back him up against the wall. I decide now that since his eyes are covered he won't have to face the wall. He won't know when I fire. He'll only hear and feel the bottle caps bite into his skin, and if I miss, he'll hear them buzz past his ears.

He stands there blindfolded, his head tilted upward as though he's trying to sneak a peek.

I walk back counting twenty paces. I hold my musket between my legs, pull back on the rubber bands, load, and aim.

'What is this called?'

'Firing squad,' I say and close one eye.

I bite down on my tongue as I concentrate, all along thinking of the bottle caps as real bullets. The machine gun in my hand. Ricardito isn't my friend anymore, but my father. I hear my father's voice talking about how he wants to leave the country, take me out of it before the government brainwashes me into thinking my own father is my enemy.

My father, tall and thin, learns to study the bullet marks on the walls. He says they tell tragic stories. A whole calligraphic record of those who've been shot, disappeared, for telling the truth about corrupt governments.

An old fashion firing squad like the Spanish used with their shiny muskets. With their conquests. With all that rancor and rage in their hearts.

'What's taking so long?' Ricardo speaks and breaks my concentration.

I take aim. My trigger finger trembles against the nail, then steadies, and I open fire.

Lalo's Skin

My FATHER and his friend, Lalo, worked together as window washers at the Colgate Building in Madrid, Spain. Lalo arrived in Los Angeles a year after we did, and never worked another day in his life. This is what my parents, many years later, before my father died, said about a man I remembered most for his skin condition than for his chronic lies.

In 1974 he mingled with other Cuban exiles at Alvaro's garage, where men talked about going home, a thick longing in their voices, spitting out their words. Alvaro, the garage's owner, liked having these guys around because they brought him business, and it was the only place at that time in Los Angeles where Cuban men could go and relax, shoot the breeze, discuss cockfights in Las Villas, killing pigs for Christmas, dancing the night away when they had been young; *jóvenes. Qué buenos días.*

They met Saturday mornings to wash their cars and fix odds and ends. Those were the days when my mother and father bickered about spending too much money on insignificant repairs. Broken door handles, noisy mufflers, loose trim.

My mother wanted our 1965 Dodge Dart to run just well enough for my father to take her to and from work, but nothing more. She didn't care if the paint lasted, or if the tires were shiny black doughnuts.

My father, though, took pride in knowing his care looked and ran clean. *Suavecito,* he liked to say.

I always accompanied him to the garage and in the afternoon he took me to bat around some balls at the park. He'd bat and I'd catch flies in deep left field where the grass was tall and the gopher holes tripped me up. Bugs stuck to my socks and bit my legs.

I liked the garage because I could always drink Coca Colas and eat those Mrs See's apple pies in the vending machine. Music blared in one of those eight-track players: Pérez Prado mambos or Orchestra Aragon's 'Cachita' or *'El Bodegero.'* Or Alvarez Guedes' taped jokes. The men laughing at jokes about *Gallegos* and Puerto Ricans.

When they were not washing their cars, the men gathered in the shade and talked about Cuba. Havana right before the revolution, the sharp clothes everybody was wearing. The Tropicana Night Club, then the beaches on Sundays. Most of my father's friends had done voluntary work back in the fields of Cuba. They despised having done it on their precious Saturdays and Sundays, picking potatoes or tomatoes, cutting sugar cane. A few showed their scars. I remember Lalo's right leg, the one with the half-crescent scar from the knee to his upper thigh, thick like a rope, pink and winding. He claimed he got that scar cutting sugar cane.

It was the first time Lalo showed everybody his skin, the blotches of purple and red, bad veins, bad skin. *'La circulación,'* he'd say to the men. *'Mala.'* Bad circulation. His skin was flaking off in parts. Everybody knew that Lalo drank, the tip of his nose reddened into the classic gin blossom.

Some of the men called it *culebrilla,* a form of shingles, but that was closely related to nerve disorders, not simple skin rashes and allergies.

'That, *compay*—what you have—is *sarna,'* one man said, and then laughed. *Sarna* was a skin disease only mangy dogs got, before scratching themselves raw. Lalo's skin, on the other hand, was simply flaking off, slivers of dead skin around his eyebrows and mouth.

'Tu madre.' Lalo would then curse.

Sometimes the men got in a few games of domino, or they played poker. For money. They sat on folding chairs. Like Lalo, most of the men smoked. He kept a couple of cigarette packs in the pockets of his cotton *guayaberas.*

Lalo's clothes were always stained, even his undershirt which I could see through the linen of his shirts. Wrinkled khakis with dirt around the pocket lip. Some of the men smoked cigars, and I gagged when the smoke reached me back by the red tool cases, next to the work bench where Alvaro kept oily pieces of car engines. I kept myself busy with ratchets and bolts.

Then one fine Saturday, Lalo, my father's best friend, stopped showing up. The men asked my father what was up, but my father didn't know.

Later that afternoon we drove to Lalo's house, a stucco Spanish-style house on a palm lined street. There was little difference between this neighborhood and ours in Bell, California. Same dirty, grassless sidewalks. When the grass lawns died, people replaced them with rock and cacti gardens. Prickly pears everywhere. *Nopalitos,* the Mexicans called it. Working class neighborhoods, that's where we lived.

My father knocked on the door but there was nobody home. Nilda, Lalo's wife, kept these empty cement flower pots on the two stairs of the front porch. No flowers. I looked inside one and saw all the cigarette butts, twisted, coiled like dead grubs in the dusty bottom.

The windows were drawn, the lights out, and my father knocked a few times, then went around the back and tapped on the kitchen window with his car keys. No answer, so we left.

The next week when Saturday came, still no Lalo. Again the men asked, but my father didn't know either. None of the men worked in the same factories, so that was yet another reason why they liked to gather at Alvaro's on the weekends.

Alvaro said to call Lalo at home, see if he was there. Maybe something came up with Nilda's sister in Miami. Or maybe Teresita, Lalo's daughter, had gotten sick. Teresita was my age and though my parents said we met in Madrid once, I don't remember. My parents didn't spend much time with Lalo and Nilda in Spain.

Here in Los Angeles it was a different story. The isolation and distance from other Cubans in Miami made people bond with others from whom they would normally would shy away. Teresita was an only child, like me. But she was a girl, and I didn't enjoy playing with her.

I remember her greasy hair, her bony legs, and the way she blinked when she was nervous. We went to different schools. Her parents placed her at St Mathias, a school for girls. I went to public school, with the ruffians and the *gangeros,* as my father's friends called *pachucos* or gang members.

We'd visit on Sundays a few times and then I'd mostly watch television, the football games. Or baseball, depending on the season. Teresita kept to herself in her room. My parents didn't like me going in her room because they said it wasn't appropriate. I didn't care.

I only visited her room once and nothing about it impressed me except for a shelf stacked with books. Nancy Drew mysteries, like those in the school library, except hers were new. She liked to read, that much we shared in common. She didn't have toys, not even a radio. Her bed was pushed to one corner of the room, away from the curtained window. The window sill was dusty, a fly and a moth dead pressed between the screen and the glass.

'What's wrong with your father's skin?' I asked her.

She turned away from me and shrugged. Her dress hung over her shoulders wrinkled and scraggly. I couldn't help but feel sorry for her.

Dandruff formed a crust around his receding hair line. His epidermis couldn't resist soap, that's what I'd heard my mother say of Lalo's condition.

'Maybe it's the shampoo,' I said.

'My father doesn't use shampoo,' she said.

She walked over to her desk, opened the drawer and pulled out a picture of a dog. She showed it to me.

'That's the kind of dog I'd like to have,' she said. 'But—'

She put the picture back and slid the drawer shut.

'Allergies,' she said.

My father walked into Alvaro's grungy office and dialed Lalo's number. He stood by the entrance where Alvaro kept his women-in-bikini auto parts calendars. My father leaned into the door frame, the phone in the crook of his shoulder and neck.

Nobody answered at first, then my father got through to Nilda. I could see his face as he turned it first toward the men, and then away toward the traffic on the street.

He said, '*Está bien*, Nilda. *Está bien*,' meaning fine, everything's okay.

Then he hung up and told the men that Nilda was crying. She didn't want to say what was the matter.

Next Sunday we visited and Lalo, Nilda, and their daughter were home. Lalo was sitting in the living room in his undershirt and a pair of cutoff pants. Part of his face was bandaged so he couldn't wear those black, thick-framed glasses he wore, the ones cloudy with smudges and dirt.

His face was shiny around his cheeks, and parts of his skin under the bandage were dark, a little purple.

My parents and I sat with them in the living and talked about Cuba. About how much work life was here in the United States. I watched television when Nilda turned it on, low volume, because she always knew how much I liked it. Either that or she read the boredom in my eyes.

'What happened?' my father asked Lalo.

Lalo's gold chain, the one with the big San Lazaro medallion, hung around the wrinkled flesh of his neck. His eyes were watery, swollen.

'The doctor'll know soon.'

'*Cancer de la piel*,' said Nilda. Skin cancer.

'Ah,' said my mother, 'that has a cure, *mi amiga*.'

'Melanoma,' said Lalo and turned to me.

Silence filled the room, laying between us like thick air, like the humidity of a rainy California Sunday.

I had a hard time watching television and keeping track of all those words in Spanish they rifled at each other. My Spanish was becoming harder to decipher, especially when Nilda and my mother talked. They spoke rat-tat-tat fast. Lots of tongue-clicking and 'r's.

Teresita came out of her room once and walked back with a glass of milk.

Nilda asked me if I wanted a glass too and some Cuban crackers with guava jelly on them.

'No, *gracías,*' I told her.

Between the Rams losing to the Redskins and Lalo's naked feet, I thought about Teresita reading in her room.

The veins around Lalo's ankles looked like the bloodworms the science teacher fed the guppies at school. Budding flowers of them around his instep, and around the sides toward his soles. His toes were long and crooked.

Lalo was telling my parents how sick he felt. Tired. Worn out. It'd been a terrible mistake for them to have left Madrid where they were all right. He didn't mind the cold. He liked the people, and the food. It was a different thing here altogether. All the work in the lamp factory, such long hours.

This was always the conversation and prelude to Lalo's asking my father for a couple of hundred dollars to pay the rent. To pay for groceries. Usually Lalo asked when my mother and Nilda went to talk in the kitchen. I guess he thought I was too wrapped up in the game to pay attention to his voice growing soft, breaking up.

'*Coño, mi socio, está de madre la cosa,*' he would say and turn toward my father. Things were really bad.

Lalo told my father he didn't know how much longer he could stand it, being sick and all.

My father sat there, leaning back against the beat-up sofa, his hands weighed down on his knees.

'I'm dying,' Lalo would finally say.

My father would tell him he'd lend him the money, and I never knew if he did so to cheer up his friend, to help Nilda and Teresita out, or both. He knew what in later years I came to know, that Lalo was a bum with no intention of ever working.

Once I asked my father out of the blue if Lalo ever worked in Madrid. My father looked up at me in the rearview mirror and he said yes, Lalo worked as hard as the next man.

'It's this country,' my father said. 'It takes it out of you.'

I had never realized the difference between this country and Spain, or the next. I was too young to know better then, I guess, but I remember that Lalo hit up my father for money several times, each time more embarrassing for both men.

I remember my mother bringing up the fact that Lalo owed my father money for years, and it looked like he, Lalo, had no intention of ever paying it back.

My father always told my mother the same thing, to forget it. *'Deja eso.'*

Later when I was in high school already, I once walked in on my father shaving and I needed to blow dry my hair because I was going out to a school dance, and I saw my father's lathered up face in the mirror, a little askew, work-worn, and I thought of Lalo's skin. All that flaking off. The veins. The clusters of them branching into dark rivers.

'Haven't you ever seen a man shave?' my father asked.

I smiled. I could hardly hear him over the noise of the blow drier. His chest looked soft, pudgy around his pecs, with the tan lines of the short-sleeved shirts he wore to work. Little red moles between patches of chest hairs.

It'd been years since we'd visited Lalo and his family. I hadn't accompanied my father to Alvaro's garage after it burned down. Rumor had it Alvaro's son burned it down so they could collect on the insurance. But that was only a rumor. Or that he blow torched it out of hatred for his father leaving his mother.

And I stood there thinking about Lalo's skin falling off his body in layers, like leaves, settling all around his feet. My mother came to call Lalo the biggest charlatan she ever knew. My father refused to ever talk about it.

For all I knew Lalo was still sitting in the same dim and grungy living room of that old house in South Gate, California, going to pieces. Moving through rooms like an unfriendly, luminous ghost.

Muñeca

THE LAST TIME I saw my father at LA General, he asked me about my mother. I didn't want to say anything because I didn't want to upset him. He'd had two heart attacks already that week, and the doctors were not hopeful he'd make it. And he didn't. What would I tell him, anyway? That my mother, still resentful of the way he'd split, burrowed deep into her room only to come out to eat? That she hung around in her *bata de casa* (her words) all afternoon and night? She kept wads of tissue in the pockets of her robe which balled up over time like the loneliness of her life? No, she was right. My father didn't need to know any of that.

I didn't tell him anything about my mother because there was nothing to say. I kept my promise to her. The other thing was that I didn't get a chance to come in early enough, before Muñeca, the woman he left my mother for, came to be with him. I snuck in twice, long enough to say hello, hold his hand like he always wanted me to, hold up the straw from his drinking cup so he could take a cold sip of water, and that was it. The last time I saw him he was dead, his eyes closed. There he lay without his glasses, the prints of the frame's little feet on the bridge of his nose. He would never cause us any more pain, I thought. I started to walk away when a nurse approached me and asked me if he was an organ donor.

I told her she'd have to ask his second wife.

'Are you his daughter?' the nurse asked.

'Yes,' I said. I was his youngest daughter of two.

'Do you think he would have wanted to donate his corneas?'

I shrugged and walked away. His wife would have to answer all those questions. My father was dead. None of us would go to the funeral. I heard later that there were three people there, two old friends of my father from work, and Muñeca. My sister Betty and her husband Bill came to visit my mother, spent the afternoon with her. I had exams to take, so I stayed in my room and studied until the early morning hours when the light of the sun came through my dorm windows and cast these long rectangular shafts of light against my bare walls.

THE FIRST TIME Muñeca came over with her second husband, I was twelve. My sister and I shared a room, though my sister was already dating a boy she met at a dance at St Mathias where we both went to school. Muñeca was married to a friend of my father's everybody knew as El Niño. They were boisterous whenever they came over. Her voice rose above everybody else's. My mother didn't like her because she said Muñeca was *chusma,* which in Spanish means cheap, low class. Sometimes she called Muñeca a *bretera,* or *fletera.* In either case I didn't know the word, but from the tone of my mother's voice I knew it wasn't a compliment.

In conversation with my sister in the kitchen, she called Muñeca *una puta.* A whore, and that word I knew, and for some reason it made me laugh because the word, so short in Spanish, rolled off my tongue bluntly, sharp. I went about the house repeating it to myself. A couple of times my mother asked me what I was saying and I'd smile at her. '*Nada,*' I told her and went back to my room.

The afternoon Muñeca and El Niño came over, my mother wasn't in a good mood. She'd argued with my father about how late he was coming home from work. The usual nonsense, as my father called her complaints, and when they fought like this, I shut the door to my bedroom and tried to study like there was nothing else going on around me.

They argued in Spanish, my mother's rat-tat-tat words bouncing off the walls: '*Hijo de puta, llegando tarde a la casa. Huevón. No sirbes para nada....*' Their voices would rise up from behind the door, and once in a while I'd open the door and shout at them that I was trying to concentrate. Who could study math? Read about the Bill of Rights, the Constitution?

'*Pueden pelearse en otro lugar, por favor?*' I would shout.

They would go into the bedroom and continue to argue in there, and then there would be silence. Toward the end of their marriage there was so much silence between my parents that everything in the house filled with it. If you picked up a vase and held it up to your ear, you'd hear the soft buzz of silence. The house became hollow with it. It was great for me because I was studying for my classes. I didn't care about anything else. My sister had her mind on her boyfriend and she herself kept out of my way. It was like having the room all to myself. Later when my sister got married and moved out and my father was no longer in the house, it was just me and my mother. Now, talk about quiet.

There were times when I had to remember to check in on my mother because the peace and quiet became so disconcerting that it spooked me, especially at night when it rained and the wind blew outside against the window. I'd open my mother's bedroom door and I'd see her asleep, her breathing rising against the bedcovers, the television casting its fuzzy snow against her outline on the bed.

THE DAY Muñeca visited, I was listening to my French lesson on tape and the tape-recorder ate up the tape and got stuck. Though I'm not at all superstitious, something told tell me that things would not go well for my parents, for my sister, me. She showed up in these hot, tight pants, with her big hips and big breasts, her hair bleached, her thick make-up.

My mother simply looked away and exclaimed: '*Alabao, mira esa mujer! Quien lo puede creer, vestida asi con su tipo de chusma, fletera enpedernida.*' I couldn't begin to translate those words.

Muñeca spoke and pronounced her words in Spanish in this vulgar way, everything innuendo. My mother called this type of pronunciation speaking with a potato in your mouth: *con una papa en la boca.*

For instance, if Muñeca said *amor* (love), she said it like this: *amol*. If she said *carta* (letter), she pronounced *calta*. A lot of exiled Cubans in Los Angeles spoke like that, and my mother hated it. When she got a case at Welfare where she worked as a social worker, my mother would go ahead and correct these women who came in talking cheap like this. My father worked there too, and he simply thought it was funny how people from other Spanish speaking countries spoke. He called it speaking like Puerto Ricans.

It was a joke he shared with some of his coworkers who were from Puerto Rico, and who were cool on the jokes.

The afternoon Muñeca arrived in our lives she put on the old records, the *salsa,* the *guaguancó,* the *son*—all this loud Cuban music my father loved, and they all danced. My father tried to pull my mother to the living room to dance with her but she wouldn't move from where she sat. It was as though somebody had glued her to the chair.

My mother sat there, her arms crossed, and looked at my father and El Niño and Muñeca dance. She danced like a slut, a *fletera,* as my mother said, wiggling her ass all over the place between my father and the other man. Her pumps were so tight the skin between her toes bulged like a lump over the leather of the shoes. She could dance though, and I stood by the hallway, and looked at her, the way she swung her arms and made all those gold bracelets she wore jingle, the way her great breasts jiggled and I thought they'd pop out of her blouse. I had never seen breasts that big. My sister's were pretty big, and my mom's. Mine hurt.

I remember the first thing my mother pointed out about Muñeca was the anklet on her left foot. My mother said trashy women wore anklets. I thought it looked nice, though it did make her ankle look thick.

They opened a bottle of rum, and my father went out to his herb garden for some *yerba buena,* and brought it back with some mint to make *mojitos*. Pretty soon they were all drunk, and they kept dancing. Since I couldn't study because my tape recorder broke, I stood by and watched. My father pulled me to the dance floor and we danced to two songs, until he stumbled and when I reached out to prop him up, he pulled me down with him.

After the fifth round, my mother got up and went into her bedroom.

My father and his friends kept dancing. When they were too drunk to stand, they sat down and Muñeca sat on El Niño's lap. She leaned into him and kissed him on the lips. When they were through, she left her lipstick smeared all over his lips. He looked like a clown.

'*Pon algo suave,*' El Niño told my father. To put something soft on.

'I'll do it,' Muñeca said and got up. She walked over to the stereo console and looked through the records. When she bent over, El Niño pointed at her ass as though to tell my father to look. They both laughed. My father cut a glance at me to let El Niño know I was there, to be more respectful. But they were too drunk and they once again started to laugh.

Muñeca found a Benny Moré record and put it on. As she did so, the needle scratched the record a couple of times. When the music started, she danced over to my father and reached out a hand to lift him out of his chair. And they swayed to the rhythm of the music. El Niño looked at them with a pleased look on his face. A wisp of his long black hair he used to hide his baldness fell in front of his drunken eyes. He was fading.

My father and Muñeca danced real close. They both knew I was standing in the hallway looking at them dance.

THE SECOND TIME Muñeca showed up at the house, she came with my father. You should have seen the look on my mother's face. It was a bad day all around. My pet parakeet got its leg stuck and broken between the bars of the cage. I squeezed my hand inside the cage where it was flapping its wings wildly. When I grabbed it, it bit me hard on the skin between my thumb and pointing finger and drew blood. I saw a drop of blood rise and cover the bite mark. I let it go, and the bird dropped to the bottom of the cage and panted.

I spoke softly to it to calm it, and at the same time, I sucked the blood, erased it from my hand. Soon enough another drop surfaced.

The bird dragged its broken leg around the circular, gravel-filled bottom. When I brought the cage out into the kitchen, I found my mother drinking a glass of water. My father was in the living room with Muñeca. I told my mother about the bird, and she put the glass down and looked at it. 'What did you do to it?' she asked.

'Nothing,' I told her. 'It broke its own leg.'

My mother gave me a stern look of disbelief. Her hands shook. She saw me notice and dropped them into the pockets of her robe.

'It caught its leg on the wires of the cage.'

'BETTY,' my mother called to my sister. 'Let's go.' Then to me, 'We're taking the bird to the vet.'

'I want to go, too,' I said.

'No, stay here with your father.'

My sister came out of the bathroom where she had been washing her hair, and in a flurry of complaints, she got dressed and left with my mother. I stayed home and looked in on my father and Muñeca.

Muñeca was crying because something terrible had happened. She'd kicked out El Niño because she'd caught him with another woman.

My mother hated Muñeca for her obvious lack of education and culture, for her selfishness and bullshit. *Esa come mierda,* my mother called her.

How could a woman live with a man like El Niño? Muñeca had grown to hate his vulgar moves, his raging about life in exile. She wanted to live the now, you know, live as best as she could in this country. Who cared about the shitty politics of a little, insignificant island?

That's the story my father tried to tone down as he told it to me. He, El Niño, didn't respect his home. My father, Mr Respect-The-Home.

'He's your friend too,' I told him.

'Sure, he's my friend,' he said. 'But she came to me.'

Sure, I thought, she came to you.

They stood in the living room where a few weeks earlier they had danced, drunk, and El Niño had sat there watching them, the way I was now. Fake, I thought, of Muñeca's tears. My father held her in his arms.

After she calmed down a little bit, he told me that they were going back to Muñeca's apartment. That he was going to help her clean up a bit. Apparently El Niño had made a big mess as he threw things around.

'When your mother comes back,' he said, 'tell her where I've gone.'

When my mother came back with the empty cage—the bird didn't make it, so she said—she didn't even bother to ask where my father was, and I didn't feel like volunteering the information. I thought about my dead bird, the last pet I would ever have.

That night my sister went out on a date with her boyfriend. The first time she came to my mother's room and asked her if she could go out, and my mother didn't say yes or no. She simply sat on her bed and stared at the *telenovelas* on the TV.

My sister told her she was going out and left. That simple.

I wished at that moment I could go with them, but I didn't brave the question. Besides my sister and her boyfriend took off fast. I went to my room and thought of calling a friend at school, but then I didn't want to talk to anybody. In that way, I was like my mother.

LATER THAT NIGHT, my father didn't show. My mother watched television until ten then fell asleep because she had to go to work the next day. I had done my math homework, though I couldn't concentrate thinking about all this activity going on in the house. Neither my sister or my mother explained to me what happened to the bird.

I sat around on my bed, feeling pretty tired when the front door opened and I heard my sister and her boyfriend come in. Initially I thought I was my father coming back with Muñeca, but it was obviously my sister because I heard her voice say something to her boyfriend. I heard her come into the room.

'Is mom awake?' she asked me.

'No,' I told her. 'And I'm tired too.'

'Good,' she said. 'Get some sleep.'

My sister closed the door and returned to the living room. I leaned back on a couple of pillows and closed my eyes. It was after two, and I knew that for the first time my father would not come home.

Then there was a great silence in the whole house and my sister had not returned to the room. Her bed was empty.

I got out of bed slowly as if I knew not to make any noise. Instinctively, I had learned to walk quietly around the house. Why make noise? I walked out of the room, and I peeked into the living room.

I found my sister sitting on the couch with her boyfriend. They were kissing, and her boyfriend had his hand under my sister's blouse. My sister's face was red from so much kissing. His was too. He kept grabbing at her breasts. I looked long enough to see my sister open her eyes and she looked at me. She saw me looking. I stood there and didn't move.

Her boyfriend cupped one of my sister's breasts and brought it out from under her blouse. He lowered his head onto it and kissed her white flesh. That's when I turned around and snuck back into my room. I climbed back into bed and covered myself with the blanket. I could hear my own heavy breathing as though I had been the one doing something I was not supposed to. I turned to bury my face in my pillow, but all I could do was listen to the flutter of my own heartbeat right there, a faint ringing between my ear and the pillow cover.

THE NEXT DAY my father still didn't come home. My mother went to work. My sister and I went to school. We came back. We each tried to avoid running into each other because I knew what I had seen, and she knew what she had been doing with her boyfriend. My mother got home, changed, and locked herself in the bedroom. It was up to my sister and me to make a couple of sandwiches. My sister made me a peanut butter and jelly, peeled a banana for herself, and opened a bag of potato chips. We ate quietly in the kitchen. When the phone rang, my mother answered before my sister could reach up to grab the kitchen phone.

We sat there and ate. Our mother started screaming into the phone in her bedroom. Betty looked across at me, her eyebrows raised. Our mother was telling our father not to bother coming back. She didn't want him in the house anymore.

'You think she means it?' Betty asked me with a mouthful of food. She drank it down with a swig of milk.

'I don't know,' I said and took another bite of my sandwich.

'It's over,' my sister said.

I didn't know what to say, but I thought *Why not?* Let it be over between them. Perhaps my mother would be back to being a normal mother again.

'I'm glad he's not here,' Betty said, 'or could you imagine the fight?'

I nodded my head yes.

Suddenly the door to my mother's bedroom flew open, and my mother stormed into the kitchen. She was dressed in a pair of pants, a shirt, some slippers. She looked at us as she went straight for the garage. She went into the garage and came out with two suitcases which she banged against the kitchen table as she passed us on her way back into the room.

She slammed the door.

We heard her opening and closing drawers, the closet, removing his shirts, his pants, all his belongings. We imagined her every move. When it grew quiet we knew she'd stuffed all of our father's clothes and bathroom trinkets into each suitcase.

Then the door opened again, and she asked my sister to go in. Betty wiped her hands clean on the tablecloth and went inside the bedroom. A while later each of them came out rolling a suitcase. I got up and out of the way. I followed them both to the front door. They rolled the suitcases out to the curb where my father always put out the trash.

My mother came back and on the way in she smiled at me.

I almost said, 'Good for you, mother,' but I held back. I kept getting out of the way because all that afternoon and evening my mother moved about the house with the most energy I'd ever seen in her. She cleaned up, swept, stuffed more of my father's things into those black trash bags and kept walking out of the house to drop them off at the curb.

'The trash comes by tomorrow,' my mother said to us.

We didn't know if she meant the actual trash truck or my father.

I merely wanted to know if my father was all right.

The next day when we left to go to school, everything was gone from the curb.

My father didn't call for a few days. Then one afternoon after I came home from school (my sister had stayed after school), I found him sitting in the living room with a drink in one hand. Maybe his second or third drink.

'Maggie,' he said to me and stood up.

'Hello,' I said.

He came over and hugged me, spilled a little of the drink on me. We stood in the living room. Him with his arms wrapped around me; me smelling the day's work on him. My father always smelled of carbon paper, also the ink of those markers gang boys use to scribble graffiti on the school desks.

'Perdoname, corazón,' he said to me. More often than not, when he spoke Spanish to me, I didn't know what to say. But I felt his weeping, now, against his chest. I really didn't know what to say other than to tell him why didn't he come back home.

'I have to leave,' he said, 'before your mother gets home,' and he pulled away from me. He returned to the kitchen to drop the glass off in the sink. He started to walk out of the kitchen, then returned to the sink, opened the faucet and washed the glass.

'No evidence,' he said and smiled.

'Stay,' I said.

'I came by to see you, and to pick up some papers I needed.'

He left quickly, missing my mother's arrival by two minutes.

When she got home, she couldn't tell he'd been there because I straightened the cushions of the chair where he'd sat. I cleaned the sink where he'd washed his drink glass, and I sprayed jasmine air freshener to cover the smell of the markers. My mother went straight to her bedroom and closed the door.

It was during the Summer Olympics in Los Angeles that my father and mother got divorced. I remember because my sister and her boyfriend watched a lot of the games on the television in the living room. He was a big sports fanatic and he'd managed to convince my sister that the Olympics was the coolest thing to watch. Of course what they spent most of the time doing was making out. I caught them a couple of times, and a couple more after I didn't care anymore what they did or didn't do in front of me.

My father didn't come by anymore, but he'd call and I learned to answer. One time I called him from a pay phone at the mall and Muñeca answered. Her voice surprised me at first when I recognized her.

'Maguita,' she said, *'cómo estas?'* I hated it when she called me La Maguita. It reminded me of all her bracelets, her thick, heavy makeup. Her raspy tone of voice. I could see her standing there, one hand on her big hips, the other holding a lit cigarette and the receiver.

'Could I speak to my father, please?'

'Eee padre tuyo is too much,' she said, trying her English, mangling the pronunciation of much into *mush.*

And when she put my father on, I asked him what was she doing over at his place. He laughed nervously into the phone.

'She visits me,' he said.

Visits, I thought. He asked about my sister. I told him she was fine. That she was seeing a lot of her boyfriend. I don't know why I said that—it just came out.

'I'll have to meet this boyfriend,' he said.

'Sure,' I said. 'Maybe we can all go out.'

'I'd like that.'

My sister and her boyfriend came out of the store and headed to where I was using the phone. 'Gotta go, Dad,' I said.

'Bye, sweetie,' he said and hung up first.

'Who was that?' my sister asked.

'A friend.'

Her boyfriend walked away into another clothing store. That's all he was, I thought, a pretty boy looking for ways to stay a pretty boy. I couldn't figure out what my sister saw in that guy.

AND THEN my sister got pregnant. She and my mother got into a big fight. My mother reverted, as she always did, to name calling: *'Ese muchacho no tiene pelos en sus…sus piernas todavia!'* She wanted to say balls, but opted for legs instead. My mother liked to scream, and I often wondered if it was because she couldn't hear.

My sister took off with her boyfriend. She said she was going to ask our father for money and then she was going to Miami to live with one of our uncles. Great, I thought. If she moves out, I have the room all to myself; thinking this made me feel like she would never do such a thing.

But she did. My father gave her the money, and she took off to Miami. She dropped out of school. Her boyfriend did too, and they left one Friday morning. My mother and I stayed by the phone hoping that she'd call and say she didn't mean it.

She did. She meant every word of it. We actually didn't hear until a couple of months later when my father called to say Betty was all right. Uncle Ramon in Miami was looking after them. She was then six months pregnant.

My mother and I stayed out of each other's way. I made my own food, and sometimes I made something for her, but she said she was having all-you-can-eat lunches at work and was not hungry when she came home.

I came home from school every day and took walks around the neighborhood. Don't ask me why. I felt like it because every time I did so, I realized that time was running out. That my sister was going to have a baby. That my father had called to say he and Muñeca were getting married. That my mother would never come out of her room. Her depression, as I came to know it. She wouldn't admit it.

I was trying to concentrate, and I realized during those walks that my own way out of this house, out of this stinking neighborhood was to go to college, and so I went to see a college counselor at school, and she told me that to get there I had to do well on the tests. I knew I had to bear down, do well, and for my senior year, I studied really hard. Took advance placement classes so that if I scored four or higher I'd come in to college with credits already finished. And so I got there.

I WROTE to my sister that I was going off to college in Arizona. She wrote back to ask what I planned to study, and I wrote back to say I didn't know, though I wanted to study something peculiar like anthropology, or geography. A counselor had told me that the best I could do with meteorology was get a job on the news. You've seen those pretty women in front of those satellite-taken snapshots of bad weather over the United States. I was to be one of those women.

I SAW my father and Muñeca a final time before my father died, before I went off to college. He picked me up to take me to a dinner and a movie. He and Muñeca came in his car. I sat in the back and looked out beyond them in the front, through her made-up poofy hair. They both smelled fresh, over-perfumed and over-cologned. My father said Muñeca was taking good care of him. He even showed me his manicured finger nails. Smoothed. His cuticles trimmed, the moons of his nails shiny.

He liked to call her *Cielito Lindo,* like the song. Muñeca brought out my father's tender side, and how she did what my mother could never do would forever be a mystery to me. Some women could do that to men.

She still wore the loud outfits, the tight pants, the low-cut blouses that exposed her cleavage, her number one asset, I thought. But my father was the happiest I had ever seen him, and we had a wonderful time, even if we didn't say much of great importance, or anything lasting, to each other. We ate, drank, made small talk, and went to the movies, which was perfect.

We ended up seeing An *Officer and a Gentleman.* Muñeca said she had a crush on Richard Gere. She even managed to pronounce his name right. *Gere.*

MY FATHER bought me a computer when I went off to Arizona. It cost him a lot of money, it was a Zenith dual 5 ¼ floppy. He insisted

I take one, that he'd heard everyone of his colleagues at work talking about how everyone in ten years would be using one. I accepted the gift and took it with me to the dorm.

I kept in touch with my mother, though our conversations never went beyond the everyday Went-to-Work-Came-Home. My sister kept sending me pictures of the baby, of his crawling around, of his standing, of his first steps. She asked when I would go to Miami for a visit.

I started dating men myself, but never long enough to have them mean anything to me. Sure, I slept with them. I enjoyed our trysts, but that was it. Call it a promise I had made to myself long ago, not to get too deeply involved. And I knew what had happened to my sister would not happen to me because I went straight for the pill. And still I made sure each guy put on his condom. If they blabbered on about how they didn't feel right, I kicked them out. Fuck them. It almost sounds like I'm an angry young woman, a popular term amongst the college professors, but fuck them too. I just know what I want and I'm going to get it.

MY MOTHER kept living in the same house in Los Angeles after my father died. She never went to visit my sister, though Betty says that they now talk to each other on the phone. Sometimes I imagine my mother getting up one sunny morning, opening the curtains to her dimly lit room, having the sunlight flood her room so that she has to close her eyes or turn away, and her saying to herself: *shit, what am I doing here? With my life? Move,* I want to hear her say. *Get the hell out of here.*

Start living, *mujer.* Start living again!

AFTER my father died. After my mother moved down to Miami to live in the garage-converted-into-efficiency behind my sister's house, I considered moving to Miami myself. But I stayed on in Tucson. I liked Tucson. I fell in love with the desert, its richness disguised in simplicity. I fell in love with the monsoons. Ah, monsoons. You think of India, some other places in Asia, but the monsoons in Tucson are famous for showing up at your doorstep one day.

If you get stranded under an overpass, good luck, the flash floods are likely to take you down with the surging currents.

If I had to choose natural disasters, I'd choose the monsoons, and if I had to name them, I'd name them Muñeca. I'd name every single one that.

ONCE in Florida, during a visit, I was eating dinner with a friend at La Carreta in Hialeah, and I got up to go to the bathroom, and to do so you have to enter the lounge area, a smoky dark cavern modeled after those underground tapa bars in Madrid where at night the Flamenco dancers put on their show. I saw Muñeca again.

My father would have said it was a small world.

Muñeca sat at the bar working on her vermouth. I knew it was her because I looked down, and there, the anklet caught the light when she moved her foot.

A man she was with kept his head buried in her breasts. He was drunk. She looked wasted herself, old and haggard.

The smoke of a burning cigar coiled in her hair. For a minute we exchanged glances and I thought she recognized me.

I looked at her long enough to make sure it was her, that she'd seen me. I thought of my father and his friend El Niño, and that afternoon they got drunk and danced in the living room of my mother's house. I thought of my mother looking out at them, and she now alone in the back room of my sister's house, the Spanish *telenovelas* on the television, watching as bad things happened to good people. Like we were supposed to go under each time, go under the weight of so much hardship, so much bullshit.

Me, I decided long ago not to get involved, not to let these seeds take root, even in the fertile darkness of my memory.

Mangoes

THEY FALL. Rot on the grass. Shadows pass over them when the afternoon storm clouds roll in the Miami skies. They lay eaten by ants, these red-orange orbs half-buried against the green stillness of the neighbor's yard. Feral flocks of Quaker Parakeets come through, waddle over to the fallen fruit, riddle the mangos' flesh with beak marks. These gray-green birds stuff their crops and fly off to feed their young in some distant tree nest like the ones in the Baptist Hospital garden. Iguanas scurry from the croton bushes to nibble at the fruit; a dominant male holding his ground near the freshest-fallen.

At night, crickets quiet each time a mango thuds against the hard-packed earth under the tree. Or are all these creatures simply swarming for a sweet taste of the fruit? Even frogs cease to call out for rain, hidden in the v-folds of palm trees and the plantain fronds by the side of the houses. In the mid-morning humid air, the mangos smell sickly sweet, even those mostly rotted through already.

This is Coral Gables, the old neighborhood where I grew up. Amazing that this kind of tropical wildlife still exists here. I am mowing the back yard in a back and forth motion. The cuttings keeps me dazed in the morning heat, the mower's throttle vibrating in my hands. I count the fruit hanging closest to the fence. Lots of mangos. Those fallen on my side I bend over, pick up, and toss into the shade of the fern bushes along the fence.

It's a small backyard, my mother's, so it's a quick job. Even so my shoulders feel sunburned already. Sweat covers my back, chest, and forearms. My hands shake still from the running engine.

I cut the engine, roll the mower up the side of the house and into the penumbra of the garage. I walk inside the coolness of the house, remove my clothes in the kitchen, and walk naked to the bathroom.

Damn heat, I think as I stand in front of the bathroom mirror, by the leak-stained basin, shaving in the single 40-watt bulb's dull light, cutting myself as I usually do from dragging the blade so close to the skin. The small birthmark on the left side of my jaw bleeds every time I cut too close to it, its trickle pink in the shaving foam.

Outside the window, I can see the mangos on the tree. They hang from a single thin stem, the fruit's weight bowing each branch. Most of the fruit is already ripe, reddened on the topside closest to the stem. In the afternoon sun they seem to glow. The faintest breeze claims a couple each time. On the floor, fallen and littered about the trunk of the tree, they form a circle of softened, pock-marked fruit, in different stages of decomposition. Ants feast upon them, surely. It is the ants that attract the lizards. Chameleons flash the skin of their throats inviting the females to take notice.

Flies, too, swarm the fruit. These mangos support a whole ecosystem in the neighbor's yard. Mother's old neighbor, Dulce, who'd passed away a couple of years ago. Or was it last year? All of mother's recently dead friends and acquaintances, who could keep track of so many? My mother did. She did so as though she were keeping track of the score. As though she wanted to know how close death was drawing to her. All her friends. All her family now gone. She was the last to die.

The house next door belonged to Dulce, a nice lady without much family. A Cuban woman herself who came to the United States before the Revolution in 1959. My mother always talked about Dulce. For the men and women of my mother's generation, history was divided into the *'antes'* and *'despues'* of the Revolution. The before and after.

A young, attractive woman lives in that house now. She comes and goes dressed in high-powered business suits, skirts and matching blazers, drives a sporty Mazda, tends to come in and out too fast, her bumper scraping the sloped edge of the driveway.

She's early to rise and gets home at the same time every afternoon, her longish hair as neat as when she left in the morning. Sometimes she brings her briefcase out of the car, sometimes she doesn't.

In the afternoon she goes out for a walk dressed in sweat pants and a t-shirt, her hair tied into a ponytail. She returns home via the same side of the street she walked away. In the kitchen she cooks quickly, probably something out of a frozen box, eats alone while reading a magazine, walks up and down the hallway to answer the telephone. She washes the dishes while listening to a Cuban radio station, but she looks too young for that. She never looks up, never, and I stand on my side of the glass sliding door that leads to the patio, which is right across her kitchen window and stare at her. But she never looks.

She's got the saddest look. Hers is the face of a woman who perhaps got married too young, divorced after a year or two, and now lives her days asking herself: what now?

In the middle of the night when she cannot sleep, she leaves the television on. The blue light flickers behind the curtains, flooding her living space, spilling out into the early morning hours. Maybe she falls asleep on the couch. Maybe she dreams between fits of waking and falling asleep.

All the while the television snows light onto her face, her closed eyes.

I SHAVE and think all I'm doing is projecting, though I myself never got married young, and am not divorced. My name is Rafael Ruiz, named after my father and my great grandfather, the Ruiz's of Oriente, Cuba. The Ruiz's of *El Almacen Oriental* fame, the market/*bodega* everyone knew. I remember pictures of my father and uncles standing in front of the place. My grandfather in his *guayabera* with an arm over each son.

Or the men and women, the *guajiros,* peasants, by the fruit stands in front of the market door. Mangos galore. *Mameyes. Guayabas. Guanabanas. Anones. Carambolas.* You name it, they had it.

When was that? *Antes?*

I've come to Miami from Boston to settle my mother's estate, this small pocket of land, this tiny stucco house filled with mother's belongings. I've been in this house for too many days now, and I have not accomplished any packing. Several dozen boxes lay flat between a kitchen chair and wall, folded neatly the way they come from Office Depot. It's overwhelming is what I think, all this stuff to pack, to discard, to throw away. I don't have the heart for it. Don't know, to be quite honest, where to begin.

Here I am, a divorce lawyer, a man too used to telling other people to divide things, split them up, sell everything, get out while they still can, and start their lives over again. The old stupid saying: it's never too late. Is it?

I should be used to all this by now, the coming and going, how people walk out for good. This country is full of gypsies. This culture of leaving. What helps me advise people on these matters has nothing to do with why I'm not packing my mother's life for a final time. It's not that at all. It's simply that by doing so, I'm packing bits and pieces of my own. Like these ceramic fish my parents picked up while on vacation in Mexico. They took a cruise, brought back so much junk with them. For days after that trip my father glowed as he showed off all the little trinkets they bought: the stuffed *mariachi* frogs, those wall plates with images of Aztec pyramids, ashtrays, an apron, bottles of tequila they never opened or shared with friends.

I rinse the foam off my face, watch the white gobs of shaving cream and cut hair whirl down the drain. I step into the shower, open the squeaky faucets, and a spurt of cold water hits my back. It's not hot enough, and I don't care. I shower quickly, lathering first, then shampooing my hair. My shaved face stings with the shampoo. I put my head under the shower, close my eyes to the mildewed walls and ceiling. In no time, I'm done. I step out slowly, dry myself, wrap the towel around my waist and walk into the cooler hallway of the darkening house.

Yellowed with age, the pictures are everywhere, hung behind dusty frames. My mother's collection in the hallways. She loved picture frames, I think, perhaps more than the pictures themselves.

I no longer have any connections to this place. Not a one, and the memories are few and far between, but those that linger, refuse to let go. My old man talked to me about those mangos falling in the next door neighbor's yard. Dulce, the woman who lived next door, would let him come over and knock down as many as he liked. He knocked down a couple of baskets for her, and she made marmalade, which she brought over in Tupperware containers for my father to eat. The old man had a sweet tooth. He ate the dessert with a wedge of cream cheese. He liked mangos like this, not as fruit, he said because as fruit they didn't taste anything like the mangos in Cuba.

All Cubans are always saying that: nothing ever tastes as good, or as delicious, or as sweet as what they ate or grew in Cuba. It's what made my father charming, I think, and it's also what got to his heart in the end. My father died one afternoon watching a baseball game. He reached over for a glass and had a massive coronary. Died instantly, the paramedic said. Instantly equals painlessly, right?

I feel like a ghost here, like I'm the one who is absent. This house of hot rooms like crazy longing. I've been down here longer than I've needed to be. Sometimes I find it hard to breathe, and when I lay on the bed my parents slept in, under the air current of a ceiling fan, it's even harder. It seems this house doesn't carry air well. It's stuffy, heavy, old air. I've opened the windows. It's how the Spanish music floats over from the house next door.

Sometimes I close my eyes. Sometimes I keep them open long after it's grown completely dark inside the room.

'IT'S YOUR TURN,' my brother says on the phone from Atlanta where he lives, 'to handle this final matter.' He's trying to disguise impatience in his voice by clearing his throat with a low guttural cough. Or he simply pronounces his words slowly.

I am the oldest of three. My sister came to stay with my mother during the last months of her illness.

Sarita came from Cleveland where she helps her American husband, Daniel, run a Subway sandwich franchise. What they call a franchise, anyway, which to them is only two stores. She manages one, he the other. They never see each other, that's what I hear. She spends her days in the back office interviewing job applicants, firing them for doing things like putting too many olives in a sandwich. Everything is counted; everything is measured.

When my mother died, I flew from Boston. A bad day to fly all around. The plane took off almost vertically. The pilot said we had to take off like that because of the limited space. I thought it was the bad weather. Three hours later, still stormy, I arrived in the Miami heat. The airport is not too far from where mother lived in the Gables.

We all gathered for the funeral, a quick affair at Caballero Funeral Home, the Cuban funeral home, well, Cuban-owned and operated at one time, the time of my parents when I remember my father and mother always getting dressed up to go to somebody's funeral. My father with his cuff-link collection. His silk ties. His *guayaberas* now hung in the closet inside their cleaners plastic. They hang there, ghostly in their starched uselessness. Mother never threw anything out. After the old man died, she kept it all. Once she said she was going to pack it all and take it to the church so they would send it to Cuba, after last year's hurricane.

After the funeral, everyone left to their own homes, to their own families, in their separate States. My brother, Frank, makes his home in Atlanta, not too far from the university where he teaches, and being the closest to the south, he'd come often, then report on mother's condition, which worsen during a bout with pneumonia this summer.

It is the middle of July now. The heat is thick, and these old window unit air conditioners don't circulate enough cool air.

'You've grown soft,' my father would say each time I came home from college and I cut the lawn in spurts because I had to stop to drink cold water. I stood on their porch and panted like a dog. He'd bring me lemonade my mother made extra sweet, lots of ice. The glass sweated in my hands while I gulped the lemonade down.

That wasn't so long ago, I think, and fill a glass with water. I have been down here now for five days. I don't know what to do, or rather where to start. My wife Kate has stopped calling. I call her now instead when I think there's something new to tell her, but there is nothing, and I have to take little action to settle things. Where to begin? No forward momentum.... Where to *fucking* begin?

I walk up and down the hallways thinking, my bare feet on the hardwood floors, a litany like the falling of the mangos in the neighbor's yard.

When my parents sold the old house, the big house where we all grew up in Kendall, my father bought this little house from an American woman who died, and her children sold it to my parents cheap. Real cheap. We'd come home and visit in this strange, small house of creaking floors, cracked walls my father constantly caulked and repainted. The mildew grew in the bathrooms. If you only ran one window air unit, the rest of the house remained a sauna.

Miami's mugginess, who could take it for so long?

All the Cuban old folk are dying. I have a friend in Boston at the firm who keeps telling me that soon there won't be any Cubans left in Florida. That Disney will have to reinvent them—a 'Cuba Land,' magical, adventurous, rum & Coke ready. Castro's still in power. My entire life Castro has been in power. He's buried six American presidents except for Clinton, who'd be better off moving to and living in Europe. Only there might he get a chance to rest. All this trouble with women. Serves him right, Kate reminds me once in a while.

My mother's house is filled with the broken memories of our passing. Of our exiled lives, though none of us feels like an immigrant anymore. Or like we live in exile. We've become assimilated. We live in the mainstream of American society.

I shouldn't have come down. Kate advised me against it. She's American of Irish descent. We met in college. We got married soon after. We have no children. We like the simplicity of our lives in Boston. She took me to Boston after we graduated from law school, and I've stayed up there until now, my blood so used to the cold. To snow.

Initially it was hard to get used to the snow. All that snow everywhere. What a pain to get the car started, and while driving, not to slide and sideswipe another vehicle on the slippery roads. But like everything, I got used to the snow. I am used to it all right. Which is the reason why this heat in Miami is doubly difficult to bear.

I am a stranger in this house too. I walk in and out of these musty rooms, recognizing what I remember of my parent's lives as perpetual exiles. In the closet the suitcases my parents brought over. Once my father tried to throw them out, and my mother got in his way, held on to the handles and would not let him out the door.

'Para que tu quieres esta basura, vieja?' he said and tugged at the suitcase. What would she want with this garbage?

My mother held on, yanked and pulled until he let go.

Or if he'd so much as touched them she'd know. It was as if those suitcases were part of her flesh. If he tugged on them, she'd sense it, even from the kitchen.

Kate hasn't given me an ultimatum yet, but I know one is coming. Two days ago I spoke to Franky, so much silence and static on the line.

'What's taking so long, Rafa?' he asked.

'All this stuff,' I said. A thick quiet. 'They were great hoarders. When was the last time you looked in the garage. There are boxes from floor to ceiling.'

'Shoot, hire somebody to come and clean the stuff out,' he said. 'There are companies that'll do that.'

Frank the realist, the quicker-picker-upper. This is the same man who grins up at me in the picture frame across the way. He's eight in the picture, freckles on his face, his front teeth not half way out.

'Listen, I'm the one who's down here. Give me a break.'

'It's up to you, brother.'

When he says 'brother,' Frank's old Miami accent still rings through, as in *bro-der*. It's the only trace of having lived down here.

'You know how long you need to stay.'

He is right, I think. I feel stuck to this wooden floor. My feet make this tiny suction noise as I walk because of the sweat I drip everywhere.

'I can't let all this stuff go. Some of it is valuable.'

'Separate the good things, put them aside, take them with you,' Frank said and cleared his voice on the other end. 'I certainly don't want anything. Mom already gave me what she thought I should keep. Each time I went down, she loaded me up.'

'You didn't take enough,' I told him.

'I took what she gave me. What she wanted me to have.'

Probably mother pushed things on him, things he didn't want anyway, or threw out as soon as he got back to Atlanta.

'There's pictures. Jewelry. Clothes,' I said.

I parted the curtains and looked out at the street. School was out. It was hot and the kids walking home from school looked tired, dragged themselves home. No rain in the forecast. Actually, it hadn't rained since I arrived.

'Do what I tell you,' Frank said, 'and call one of these places.'

I told him I'd look into it all right. The phone book sat on the telephone table in the kitchen by the door that lead to the garage. Yesterday, I had walked in there. Replaced the burnt out bulb. All these boxes stacked up against the walls. A lifetime of packing.

'You've been looking for a few days now. The sooner you empty it out, the faster the realtor can put the house up for sale.'

We never lived here as kids, that's why none of us feel any connection to this house. By the time my father and mother moved in, we were on our own. None of us felt attachment. We loved the old house in Kendall and thought fondly of our days there. Its big yard where Frank and I played flag football with our friends. We built a fort by a fallen tree in the back. We kept Sara out. Boys only, we told her. My mother would chase us out and told us if Sara couldn't be in there, neither could we.

Frank needed to go. We hung up. He hasn't called back. He probably thinks I've taken care of everything already and I'm on my way back to Kate, to my life in Boston.

I SIT on the old man's chair with the footrest, the one in which he suffered the coronary, and I look at the worn carpet. Everything looks Miami Beach cheap here. Or is it all the years past? The television console holds rows and rows of picture frames, Franky and I with our brand new Huffys the Christmas of 1972. Sarita with Mochito, her French poodle she fed pieces of chicken while it rested on its back. It ate that way, she trained it to. Chunk after chunk. It grew fat. When Sarita went away to school, my mother and father kept Mochito until it died of old age.

Faded black and whites of Franky's graduation, of Sarita's, mine from St Brandon's. The three of us on the step of our college. I ended up at Louisiana State University. There's the one of me teasing Tony the tiger from outside his cage. Those years my parents spent going from college campus to college campus. They drove to LSU and back. To Sarita's and Franky's schools they flew.

Had they not immigrated from Cuba, we could have easily believed we had lived in the United States all our lives. If our parents didn't speak Spanish to us, they could have fooled us. They could have made up the story of our being born and raised in the States. That simple.

I am sitting there on the chair when I hear a car's engine turn a couple of times and die. A door slams shut. A hood pops open. I get up and peek outside the window. It is the neighbor trying to get her car started.

I go to the bedroom, get dressed in a pair of shorts, put on a tight-fitting t-shirt, and my tennis shoes without socks. I hurry to the garage where I remembered my father keeping his jumper cables. He hung them behind the kitchen/garage door. I grabbed them and walked outside.

She's trying to turn the engine, but it clearly sounds like the battery is dead.

Walking across the front lawn, I reach her in time before she gets out. She has on an electric blue evening dress. There's a gold necklace around her neck, her nails are done. She's wearing makeup, red lipstick. Her hair is smoothed over her ears and tied in the back with a Spanish comb.

She notices my approach and smiles.

'I've got these,' I tell her and hold up the cables.

She tries the engine one more time. Uncertainty is my business, I want to say, but don't because I'm already believing I'm a fool for doing this, coming out like this.

'It's the first time,' she says, 'it does this.'

She starts to climb out when one of her shiny dark blue pumps falls out. Her white, small feet slip back in. She smiles again. Her eyes are bright. She looks like a completely different person than the one behind the kitchen window.

'Hold on,' I say and go to the rented car.

I climb in, start it, back it up and pull up to the front of her car. I pop the rented's hood. Get out. Hook up the cables to her battery first, then to mine.

'Wait until I start it,' I tell her.

'I know how it goes,' she says. 'I've had nothing but junkers before this one.' She's smiling behind the windshield.

I turn the ignition, the car roars as I step on the gas.

A few seconds later, she starts hers. Nothing to it. I get out, unhook the cables and absentmindedly throw them in the back seat of the rented car.

'Listen,' she says, 'thank you so much. You saved my evening here.'

'What are neighbors for?' I tell her and immediately feel ridiculous for putting it like that. I'm not her neighbor and she knows it.

She's never seen me before in her life. She doesn't stay up at night walking in the dark, staring at me across the way through her windows.

'What happened to Noemi?' she asks about my mother.

'She died,' I tell her.

'Oh,' she says. 'I'm sorry.'

The engine hums under the hood, sounding like it's getting plenty of juice from the recharged battery.

'She always loaned me magazines. She was a wonderful *vecina*. I'm sorry.'

Her Spanish rolls off her tongue. *Vecina.* Neighbor.

'My sister was with her.' And I want to tell this woman my mother died in her sleep, her giving out, her lungs out of air.

We stand in the sun and I feel the heat rising up from the cut grass. A thick vapor that wraps itself around my legs. Mosquitoes bite the backs of my legs in tentative landings. She's simply beautiful, I think...her sad, deep-set eyes.

'I've got to go,' she says and climbs in.

I move up on the sidewalk, away from her car. She pulls out and drives away. I stay there long enough to watch her wave goodbye as she passes. The car's right blinker goes on before she turns for good at the corner.

When I park the rented car and get back inside, I hear the phone ringing. I reach it on the last ring. It's Kate. I'm out of breath. She tells me I'm out of breath.

'Running?' she says. She knows I don't run or exercise much.

I'm holding on to the receiver, feeling the sweet drops bead down the sides of my back. 'No, I was outside,' I tell her.

'Oh, I see. You hurried in,' she says and I can hear her walking around in our own kitchen. She's got a long t-shirt on, her pajamas which she's worn since college. She's wearing socks too. Her long hair is wet from having taken a bath. She takes baths when I'm away. She showers when I'm home.

'When are you coming?' she asks quickly.

Is she eating? I think almost thinking she's chewing a piece of bread, or her nails. She chews on her nails when she talks to friends on the phone.

'I don't know,' I say and sit back down on my father's chair. The arm rest fabric feels smooth, worn, thin from the years of use.

'They called from the office today,' she says.

'What did they want?'

'They wanted to know what I knew.'

Don't tell them, I think and put my feet up. They too are sweating. The mosquito bites welt on the back of my legs, on my ankles. Begin to itch.

'When I thought you were coming home.'

There's a pause. I can imagine Kate reaching for the jar of peanut butter, which she loved to eat by the spoonful.

'When do you think you'll be here?'

'I don't know,' I tell her. 'There's all this packing. It's endless.'

If she only knew that I haven't even started.

'A couple of days? Four? A week?'

'Kate, I don't know.'

'Settle it with them. Next time I'm letting the machine answer,' she says.

I don't respond. I let the silence buzz between us.

Another pause. 'What's going on up there?' I ask.

'The usual. The Henrys have another dog. It barks in the night. Keeps me awake.'

'It's hot down here. The heat's what keeps me awake.'

'How much longer, Ralph?' She knows I hate to be called Ralph, but she thinks she's being funny. I can tell she's nervous because she knows I don't know when I'm going back.

'A few more days,' I tell her and sit up straight. 'I'll be done in a few days.'

She says she's spoken to Sarah, my sister, and to Frank and they are both concerned about why I'm taking so long.

'It's none of their goddamned business,' I say.

'You know what you need to do,' she says. 'I'm here.'

'I know that,' I say.

'Good night,' she says.

'It's afternoon down here,' I tell her. It must be cloudy there, I think.

'Do whatever you need to do,' she tells me in a fading voice as though we were moving the receiver away from her mouth, and hangs up.

I imagine my arrival at the house. I will walk in empty-handed, depleted from another emotionally-draining flight. Leaves will fall over the roof of our house, hang from the gutters, bunches of them hugging the walkway to the front door. Inside the house there will be flowers on the dining room table, magazines neatly stacked on a chair, car keys on top of the day's newspaper. I will call out Kate's name and there will be no answer. She will not be home. She will not be there for a while. I will walk through the house like a stranger, looking into the rooms for the first time, wondering who it is that lives here.

Emptiness swallows me whole. Like here. Like now.

I get up, move about in my dead mother's house, walk to the kitchen for a glass of cold water. The icemaker in the refrigerator is broken, though there's ice in the tray. I turn the tray upside down on the counter, cracking the cubes out. I grab them and drop them in a glass, fill the glass with tap water, and it tastes terrible. A metallic taste. It's the ice. I dump it out and refill it with room temperature water. Better taste. Coolness nowhere to be found.

IT IS evening now. No more sun. I strip in the heat, turn on all the air conditioner units. They kick start and hum. Rattle like a car's engine. *Junkers,* she had said, in her young voice. *Junkers.*

I walk around in the dark. Across the way all the lights are off too. The night darkens very still. There's a storm rolling in. A nasty one from the stillness in the hot air. Fronds cast shadows against the hallway lights.

How long has it been since I've eaten? My stomach growls. I can hear it churning. I feel as restless as the flickering shadows against the walls.

Now it begins to rain. I crack open one of the windows. Maybe the rain will cool everything down. When it pours, I close my eyes. I am thinking of something my father said about the way he ate mangos when he was a child in Cuba. That he'd eat them in the rain because then he didn't have to walk around with the sticky juices under his chin, neck, on his hands. It never made sense to me, the stuff about eating his mangos in the shower.

Thunder cracks in the distance. Lightning flashes in the room. I think about the distance between the sound of thunder and the lightning flash. How far, I wonder, how far. It is the middle of the night. It is raining. I cannot sleep in this house.

I GET OUT of bed. I wish I smoked. I wish I drank. I walk in the darkness of my dead mother's house, my dead father's. It is pouring outside. Across in the neighbor's house, the kitchen light is on. It is a sad light, faint. Rain shines off her window glass. I wonder where the light comes from outside.

I open the sliding door and walk outside. The rain pelts my skin. It runs down my back. The fence that separates the neighbor's yard from my mother's house is not that tall. The mango tree branches almost reach the fence. I reach out to grab a mango, but I can't. I climb the fence, heaving up as I pull my weight.

I make it over. Step across to the tree. The fruit hangs low. I can feel my way around. I pull one, then another. My arms soon load up with wet mangos. I am walking back when one of these motion sensor floodlights comes on.

I feel caught, a man driven by what he cannot have.

A man with an armload of stolen mangos.

I am surprising myself. Stuck, I freeze in the light. I will not say what I'm doing. Where I'm going, wondering all along who's going to buy it, this, my story of why I've chosen to steal all this sweet, hard fruit.

Pomelos

THIS IS THE TIME of year when my mother visits us in Tallahassee, and mostly she goes on walks by herself or with her two granddaughters. She walks in the mornings after I or my wife have taken the girls to school, or in the afternoon after the girls return.

My mother, almost sixty-three, always returns renewed with energy to begin her day with '*gusto*,' as she calls it, and a handful of azaleas or lily cups she's found and clipped from our neighbors' yards. How many times have I told her not to do that? She can get shot here. Since people wouldn't know who she is, only seeing an old lady entering their property and leaving with a bunch of their flowers.

'*Ha!*' she says. 'They wouldn't shoot an old woman. Not *this* old woman.'

She likes flowers, says she's never seen any like this back in Cuba, the place of her birth, of mine. The place of my birth exactly thirty-eight years ago, but which I've forgotten, or pretend I've forgotten, but my mother's whip-fast to remind me.

My wife and I bought this house in the woods because we wanted privacy. The last neighbor we had kept complaining of our dog's barking. That man stalked us whenever we got home from work; he'd be on his porch and then he'd see us and call out that he worked nights, that we owed him for all the time he spent awake, that he'd get a gun if he had to. . . .

We got used to it, but eventually we simply opted for the easiest solution. We put our house up for sale, sold it, and moved.

My wife and I both share a dislike for zero-lot properties, and so right before my in-laws died we moved here to this two story house on two acres in the woods, with a mossy green pond where ducks and turtles make their home. Egrets and anhingas too.

We live in a secluded cul-de-sac in the woods of Tallahassee, that's what we like to tell the family in Miami. It keeps them interested in our exotic-too-far-to-visit-us lives.

Spring is imminent now, and that's why my mother always returns to visit this time of year. Last night my wife and I discussed whether my mother had ever visited us in this time of year.

'Last time she was here was May,' my wife says. 'The gardenias were in bloom, remember?'

We've begun to measure time by how things bloom and flower around us. Our two daughters don't really care much about blooming flowers yet, except for Alex, the oldest, because like me, she is allergic to pollen. In Tallahassee pine and oak pollen take over the place in one smooth, silky-green blanket. It sneaks through the air vents in the cars and next thing I know we are having sneezing attacks.

My mother seems happy as can be, even though every once in while I can see her eyes turn to melancholy as she observes a pair of cardinals at the bird feeders. She thinks of her husband, my father, who loved birds and nature this much in bloom.

I haven't wanted to tell her about the surprise I have waiting for her and my wife this Spring when I turn the side of our pond into a garden with blooming Easter lilies, daffodils, and gladioli. Next to it will be a gazebo I've ordered and paid for, and which is being built somewhere in Wakulla—I will know it is finished when I see the truck coming down the dirt path that curves along our property. I've also asked Hank, our carpenter/handyman, to build a Japanese-style bridge over the pond. Everything will soon fall into place.

My mother visits and helps us out with the children. My wife and I worry that our girls will grow up detached from their parents' and grandparents' roots, and we could see why they would. Right here very little of the world's malice reaches them. This pond we have around our front yard is like a moat, and that's why I think a bridge will help us establish a connection with the outside, though 'outside' is everywhere in these woods, a verdant universe.

Soon my daughters will be teenagers, then they will have dates, and soon after they will be off to college. 'Not so soon, honey,' my wife likes to say to slow me down, keep me in the here and now.

We don't watch television. We don't do much of anything other than work at the university and spend time reading. Nobody visits us up here, and from town we no longer have any kind of meaningful friendships. Academia, as we've come to know it, is best kept at a distance, in part because none of it has any relevance in our personal and family life. It's a job, like any other, and since we think of ourselves as professionals, we get the job done in the workplace and return home to be parents, spouses, folks who love quiet and flower buds and the woods.

Most of our friends have gone on to other places, the way it normally happens in second-rate universities where politics and pettiness drives the best far away to other jobs and places.

My wife is a cultural critic, and every day I try to be a better poet, but lately the words haven't been kind. I'm much more interested in the daily struggle a pair of hawks have here in my yard. They have built a nest in a patch of trees in the empty lot next door and have hatched two chicks. Both of which are ravenously hungry. The hawks take turns hunting the lazy frogs around the pond; they take five or six each day. The squirrels appear to be too big for the hawks. The squirrels skip and dash with caution. You can see it in the way they ease down the trees and approach the bird feeders. They devour the see I buy all the time, and that's my war with them.

The days have started to grow longer. During a recent trip to the corner Publix, I spotted these huge orange-grapefruit things that had a sign: 'Pomelos: 99 cents per lb!'

I'd never seen anything like them, but I immediately thought of this dessert my mother makes for us when she comes to visit. A sort of candied rind in syrup. *Dulce de cascara de naranja,* that's what my mother calls it. She singsongs it to the girls and both of them stumble with the words as if they were tongue-twisters.

My mother is upset because the girls are growing up not speaking Spanish. My mother thinks Spanish is the only connection they will have back to our place in time, whatever that means. We fear she's right.

I thought *giant grapefruit,* but a grapefruit is dwarfed considerably by a pomelo. Pomelos are huge. Giants of the citrus world, I guess.

So I hold a pomelo in my hand and the produce man sees me weighing the thing and comes over. 'Pretty big, ain't they?' he says and smiles. His black, thick-thick framed glasses slide down the length of his nose.

'What are they?' I ask.

'Pomelos.'

Suddenly between us the produce sprayer comes on. They've worked it so that the sound of thunder and the flash of lights act like a lightning storm coming on, a promise of rain, and then a few seconds later the sprayers come on.

'Pomelos?' I ask.

'Let me show you,' the produce man says. He takes one of the fruit, gets a knife from under his apron, and cuts it in half.

'See?' he says and shows me both halves. 'Not an orange, and not a grapefruit. More like a mutant cross. Pretty good too.'

He cuts a wedge and hands it to me. I taste the piece readying for bitterness, but the pulp is sweet as can be. Not tart as I expected.

'One of these can make a breakfast,' he says and puts away the knife. He walks away as though he's done his good deed for the day.

I stand there thinking not so much of the sweetness of the pulp, but of the thick and meaty rind. I am thinking of my mother and how happy she'd be with these huge pomelos.

I grab six and put them in the cart. The cashier smiles at their size, and looks for the code for grapefruit. I correct her. She types in the code for pomelos and I can see her registering *pomelo* in her short-term memory. The proud finder, I take them home.

At home I walk them into the kitchen in my arms. My mother is on the phone to one of her friends in Hialeah. She is speaking Spanish like a parrot, which is what my daughters say she sounds like when she machine-guns her Spanish *rat-tat-tat* like that, a mile a minute.

She sees me *and* the fruit. She says goodbye to her friend and starts to do this noise with her tongue, a click-clopping. I know the sound too well. I grew up with it. It means she's happy. She is holding a pomelo now. 'Oh, oh, oh,' she is saying and turning the golden orbed fruit in her hand. She smells the fruit which is almost as big as her head.

Then the melancholy returns to her eyes. *'Si tu papa hubiese estado vivo,'* she says to me. If my old man were alive...?

'Que bellezas,' she says and takes them one by one from my arms and sets them up on the kitchen counter. She turns them all as if she were inspecting pickling jars.

I tell her how and where I found them and how I think they'd make her *dulce de naranja* the best ever.

'But six,' she says, 'would yield many jars of it.'

'Take some to your friends in Hialeah.'

She clicks her tongue against her teeth again. She reaches over for the kitchen knife she takes pride in keeping sharp and peels one of the fruit. I stand by watching because I know what she will say when she sees how thick and meaty the white rind is; I need her praise.

Instead, she begins to tell me the story of how this kind of fruit grew even bigger in Cuba, in the province of Las Villas where she is from. She remembers the fruit growing in her great-grandfather's orchard. Her great-grandfather was from the Canary Islands, a rosy-cheeked *'Isleño.'*

She was a little girl then, no older than Alex, and she remembers Abuelo Trino and how he'd visit all of his sons and daughters every morning and how to all his grandchildren he brought gardenia buds and jasmine flowers in his starched *guayabera* pockets. My mother tells us this story of her life in Cuba while she peels all six pomelos.

In no time she's cut out all the pulp and put chunks of it in a Tupperware container. My wife loves the sweet pieces and gorges herself on them. The girls like it too. I stand by really proud I have gotten something everybody likes. Of course I know this, like everything else, is short-lived.

There's always latent tension between us and my mother because she brings her old world with her when she visits us. My mother is the kind of person who thinks out loud, so we don't have to follow her around to know what she is thinking. Mostly what she thinks isn't what we want to hear: *how messy we are, how we are bringing up the girls allowing them to do as they wish, how they don't speak Spanish, and what a terrible disservice we are doing them by not teaching them about Cuba.*

Last year after my mother left us after a month-long visit, my wife came up with the plan to keep my mother busy whenever she visited next. My wife thinks that by keeping her active my mother doesn't tend to speak her mind so openly in front of her and the girls. Me, I've learned to take it. I remember the way she drove my father into a frenzy by criticizing him whenever he painted the house, worked on the car, planted a tomato orchard by the kitchen door.

'Those tomatoes aren't going to grow,' she'd say to him. Or 'the car isn't going to drive any better,' or 'I think the house needs another coat, around the windows...."

My wife and I argue often that my mother is the stereotypical Cuban, middle-aged woman. The nurturing mother. The perfectionist. A woman who had to live in a spotless, well-organized environment.

This is the tension between my wife and I, and is the reason why this Spring I hired a cleaning service to come to the house every Wednesday, so that my mother would not have to pick up and clean after us. I didn't expect my wife to do it, so why would I expect my mother to?

It is a sore point between us, my wife and I, and it is always better left unsaid, and shortly after my mother leaves everything in our daily life will return to normal. The girls with their messy and toy-scattered room. Us with our laundry all over the closet floors where our worn shoes have begun to look like keeled-over armadillos.

I've stopped expecting anything from life since my father died of a coronary thrombosis in a Hialeah hospital, a man who had only turned sixty-three and who'd expected to live a little longer. Not to be.

But that's another story.

This is the story of the pomelos in our lives.

Once peeled and rinsed, my mother bags all the pieces and puts them in the freezer for a couple of days so that, as she claims, the colds zaps the bitterness out of the rinds. In a couple of days, my mother has a black pot on the stove and she's boiling the rinds. She boils them for several hours, draining them of their water every three or four hours and then starts the process all over again.

It is while she is doing this that we gather around her because she seems to be the happiest, and so, lost in thought, she begins to tell us the story of her last trip to Cuba last year when she visited her ninety-year-old father.

'*Ultima vez,*' she says and stirs. My grandfather is senile and thinks now he is a poet. He is a *güajiro*, a Cuban peasant. Been so all of his life, first when he was young and worked for a sugar cane mill, and then when he went into business raising cattle for meat and milk. She brings us photos of her trips because she wants me to remember, and she wants the girls to have a connection back to the people in our lives.

Most of the photos of my relatives look the same: tired faces, much older than whatever age they are, skinny, malnourished bodies. They look as weather beaten as the corner houses, the naked trees, the ravaged landscape. Bones like bricks, skin like bleached buildings. The human body wasn't made for this kind of scarcity, for this type of lack and need. The revolution has failed us all so miserably. Nobody talks about it in the island. And here? Well, that's why we live so far from Miami, to keep away from the daily litanies.

Everybody is tired and worn out in Cuba, my mother says. Everybody has learned to live with less, with less than zero, with nothing. *Todo el mundo vive fugilateando, arreglando, buscando....*

When the girls hear her speak in Spanish they turn to me or their mother. Some things we can translate. Other things we can't, or won't. Everybody lives *rummaging, fixing, looking*...this is the daily struggle for all Cubans in Cuba. *El cocodrilo se unde. El cocodrilo se ahoga.*

Soon the smell of rinds cooking fills the kitchen, this bitter-sweet stink of orange. The girls say *na-ran-ja*, and I say pomelo to remind them of the exact name. Everything has a name. For example, '*abuela*' is grandmother, '*naranja*' is orange but not 'pomelo.'

'Smells of orange,' Gabby says. Gabby doesn't care to be exact, and I love that about her. A flower is a flower no matter its name, and a hummingbird is a bird no matter that it isn't like any other bird.

My mother tells us the story of going back to Cuba, taking with her as much as she's allowed by both the Cuban and the United States government. She takes back medicine, shoes, clothes, caps and socks for her father, my grandfather Domingo. A *sombrero* to keep the sun out of his thin face.

If angels speak Aramaic, Cubans speak in the riddles of angels. Their Spanish has become a cauldron of melting words: English, Spanish, Spanglish, Haitian, Russian. You grow up learning the words you need to voice hunger, food, clothes, medicine.

My mother tells us the story of the black woman, *'la pobre negrita del barrio,'* who was dying of colon cancer and couldn't find a single aspirin or painkiller to help her through the day. My mother brought some Tylenol for her nieces who sold them on the black market for a dollar apiece.

My mother arranged it so that Mercedita, that's what they called the black woman, would get some Tylenol. Mercedita is a close friend of one of my aunts, their history is not familiar to my mother, but she knows that people in Cuba have bonded across racial lines because they have to make do. Something like that.

I remember the black woman who lived at the corner in our neighborhood and to whom my mother took me when I became *empachado,* when I'd get a stomachache from eating too many berries, or almonds, or too much candy. Teresa was her name. Teresa the hand-healer. *La pasamano.* Who rubbed goat's fat on my belly and made gas come out of me. Teresa did this for a living, her healing. The same old story of having to make do.

We know the story. Scarcity. Lack. Need. What bonds one human to another, given the circumstances of a place, of a corrupt regime, though we are surprised that Castro's name hardly comes up at all in this story.

This is my mother's premonition story. A story about change to come. She tells us Mercedita, after my aunt Lalo gave her friend my mother's-brought-to-Cuba Tylenol, begins to come by the window of the room in which my mother's sleeping. She brings my mother flowers, orange blossoms, gardenias, *'nardos,'* any kind of wild flower Mercedita finds on her way. My mother says that Mercedita and she bonded over the Tylenols.

Alex and Gabby grow tired of hearing so much Spanish, so they go upstairs to play Nintendo. The bleeps and splats reach us below. But my mother is lost to her stirring the rind in the big black pot and she's just talking now, regardless of who is listening.

'Mercedita,' she says, 'came by every morning and called out: *'Onei-dita, Oneidita, te traigo las florecitas....'*

And when my mother opens the window, there is Mercedita with her sick-looking face, trying to muster a smile to greet my mother with. She is a young woman dying. Teeth missing like holes in her pockets. My mother has always gravitated to people dying because—and this is my idea—she likes to play doctor. She likes to diagnose people, care for them, and nurture them back to health.

She began to go for walks with Mercedita. They walked in silence because they had already talked about their lives, and so to talk about where they were, and what brought them together would bring them to politics, a subject my mother promised never to discuss while she visited Cuba.

When it was time to leave, my mother left a couple of my aunts some money to give to Mercedita so that she could buy herself something nice. After she returned, my mother never heard whether Mercedita was still alive or had succumbed to the cancer ravaging her body.

My mother says she's learned to live one day at a time. Doesn't care much about the future. Doesn't care too much what is going to happen tomorrow. Her life is in the here and now. *Aquí,* as she calls it. After my father died, she's learned to be self-sufficient. She goes out more, socializes more. Has a better time meeting her friends at social events. A wedding. A baptism and christening. A house birthday party. She knows her friends are dying. She knows people all around her are dying, leaving this place she knows called Hialeah. The land of her exile. The place of her final rest. Once she asked me to take her remains back to Cuba and my father's too. She wants to return home to live, even if it is in the afterlife.

I tell her she is being too dramatic, that she is too sentimental.

'Sentimental is good,' she says, stirring the thick pomelo stew.

I cannot help but think of the roundness of a pomelo. The filled-orb shape of it. I dream of a pomelo tree, branches heavy and sagging close to the earth. I dream of how my life is halved between pulp and rind, between emptiness and *bullicio,* or clutter as my father would call it.

I think of Mercedita—even without a clear mental picture of her—a thin, black woman dying of cancer that has no cure, not in Cuba, not in the United States, not yet anyway. She is walking with my mother entering people's gardens and taking the best of the new flowers in bloom. It is a bright and sunny Cuban afternoon. There's a soft hum in the air, then silence.

Some things are better left to silence. *'Qué silencio,'* my mother says, then wonders aloud about pomelos, those I brought her from Publix.

Her question makes me look it up on the internet. I love the internet because it always gives me something to do when the words are not coming. I type in *pomelo* and get a plethora of hits. The first two explain that a *pomelo's* species is *citrus paradisi,* a cross between sweet orange and pummelo which was initially produced in Barbados. I write some of the information down and return to show my mother.

Though she listens, she is intent on keeping her rinds stirred. Something about the way she is looking at the steam roiling out of the big pot's mouth tells me she is back in Cuba. Walking down a dirt path toward her parent's house. There is a mockingbird on a fence post. It doesn't quiet as my mother passes by.

'Tell me,' I say, 'how to make this when you are not here.'

My mother smiles and steps away from the stove. She thinks for a brief moment, then tells me.

'Está es la receta.'

Recipe for *dulce de naranja:* (or pomelo, if in season) peel and clean the pulp off the meaty rind. The meatier the rind the better and that's why the pomelo is best for this desert. Place the peeled quartered rind in a plastic bag in the freezer to aid in the removal of the bitterness, or *amargura* in Spanish, though this is not necessary. Soak peeled rind overnight in salted water. In the morning, drain, refill with cool water and set to boil for several hours. After the initial three hours, drain and add new water. Boil until the rind is soft. Drain again, then add water and lots of sugar, about a cup. As water evaporates add more sugar until sweet to taste. Once the pulp has reached a caramelized consistency, allow to cool. Jar in its own syrup juice. Serve cold with a slice of white cheese or cream cheese. Best eaten in the summer in the company of your loved ones.

Salvation

'HEAR THAT?'

'What, Rafa?' Sonny felt the burning behind his eyelids as he tried to open his eyes in the dark.

'The thunder, dummy. What else?'

'No.'

. . . In the distance thunder rolled.

'Hear it now?' Rafael's voice sounded distant, hollow.

. . . 'Yes,' said Sonny in the dark of the small bedroom he and an older brother shared. Shadows moved across the walls and ceiling. Tree branches clawed at the windows.

'Storm's coming.'

They listened to the rain falling on the banana leaves outside by the window. It hadn't let up all night. It trickled from the sloped roofs and fell over everything.

'Is he gone for good?' Sonny was referring to his father.

'Nah, he'll come back.' His brother, Sonny knew, was only saying his father would return just to cheer him up. This time he was gone for good, their father had said so himself.

'He said he wouldn't.'

'Wanna bet? Cowards always come back.' Every time Sonny thought he'd fallen asleep, Rafael broke the silence and spoke. His voice sounded so far away.

'I don't feel good,' Sonny said. His head pulsed at the temples. He thought of the dream before the storm started up. He had stood in front of a chicken carcass riddled with maggots. With a stick he built up enough courage to turn it over, holding his hand over his nose and mouth. The heat made the stink of rotting flesh waft up to his nostrils. He didn't want to gag. The maggots writhed between the sinew of flesh and bone, white slivers made whiter among so much reddened, bloody flesh. Sonny thought of how the chicken got here. It's headless corpse reminded him of a feather duster his mother used. When the wind picked up a bit, he brought his hand down because he couldn't smell the rot after a while. He'd gotten used to it.

The chicken's feathers were speckled with dried blood. Some lay flattened against the purpled flesh, stuck there by the dried-up blood. When he turned the carcass over, a knot of maggots fell out and twisted like kite string on the dirt. Confused, the worms knitted themselves into a tighter ball. Would they turn against and eat each other, Sonny thought. He'd seen this before, the times he'd gone with his father to the cockfights. One man in particular whose name he couldn't remembered showed him where they disposed of the dead rooster who'd lost and gotten killed. The man took him there and showed him the mound of bones, the carcasses, the green-backed flies buzzing over the pile. Sonny heard the *Zzs* in his ears for days.

In his dream, the chicken came alive, headless, it's bloody neck stump like a broken branch. It clawed at the earth. It scratched something there in the moist ground. But Sonny couldn't read the word. He got spooked and in the dream tried to step on the chicken, mashed it back into the land of the dead.

THUNDER broke again in the distance...The rain had come in the afternoon, Sonny remembered, when the clouds gathered and turned mean-looking with the color of lead. Gusts of wind carried dried leaves across the patio floor, hinged them against cracks and crevices. He watched the sky from the patio where he had gone the minute his father started to shout at his mother.

They argued about the same thing: when was his father going to stop coming home so late? Sonny's father gambled away all his money.

The family's money. He couldn't help it, he repeated whenever Gris worked him into a corner. Rigo spent all his time at the fighting cock pits in Matanzas.

Sonny stood on the patio among the empty clothes lines and nervous chickens in their wooden milk bottle crates turned into cages, among the rusty bicycle frames and mildewy box spring mattresses and discarded stoves, among the pungent smells of chicken shit and gasoline and oil. He stood there in the rain getting soaked and cried. The rain fell at an angle, so the roof ledge couldn't serve as shelter. The rain mixed with the spilled gasoline, forming these gorgeous iridescent rainbows that swirled and broke with every drop. The water felt warm as it soaked his short sleeve shirt and torn pants which were made out of flour sack yute.

Sonny leaned against the lime wall and remembered what his older brother Brito had told him once: a man didn't cry, and if little Sonny was a real man he wouldn't be crying like a girl all the time, like his sister Kenya. He stood in the rain and remembered, and for some reason all he was able to recall were the bad times when he'd heard or seen his father, during violent moods, hurt his mother. It was something he'd seen three times already. His father hitting his mother on her back, on the side of her head. Her bruises shone on her face for days, turning purple, then black, a tinge of charcoal under her eyes. On those nights, he was so afraid he urinated on his bed, and then the bad dreams and all his bad feelings woke him. He'd clean up in the dark, by the window so he could see how to change, and then he climbed in bed with his mother. Gris turned in fits, her flesh burning when it touched his. Her breathing softened as she fell deeper into sleep. Sonny wedged himself into his mother's belly and breast, sideways, and rested his head on the pillow. He heard the beating of his own heart, his mistook it for his blinking as he tried to see the shadows move across the wall in the dark.

Now the fever ran high. Sonny's brother, who thought Sonny had peed on the bed again, felt the high temperature on Sonny's sweaty skin that night when they couldn't sleep because of the thunder. Lightning kept flashing into the room. Sonny's flesh burned. Immediately, Rafa, as Sonny called his brother Rafael, the last older brother to remain in the house, rushed to their mother's bedroom, woke her up and told her about Sonny's fever.

Gris Manteca awoke in a panic. She'd been dreaming of her mother again, falling off the horse and into the river. Drowning. Screaming.

She was a big-boned woman with large hips, but that night she sprang from her bed as swiftly as a cat might jump from a window sill. Then ran to the bedroom and felt Sonny's forehead. Her hands felt cold to Sonny. The heat on her boy's forehead and loins alarmed her. For an instant she was lost and confused, standing there in the dark of the boys' room.

When she pulled back on the bed sheets, she saw that the boy's legs, glistening with sweat. Right there between his legs his testicles had swollen to the size of lemons. This, obviously, was not normal, she thought.

Alone, she didn't know who to turn to. It was raining hard outside, so hard that the drops hitting the tin roof of the tool shack next door sounded like the gallop of horses. Death was coming for her boy, she thought, riding on Her black stallion. Then she thought of the only person in the barrio who could help her. Josefa the healer, the *curandera,* the medicine and herb woman. *La yerbera* as people in the neighborhood called the ancient apothecary. But Josefa was too old to make house calls, especially so late at night and in such bad weather.

But time was too important and Sonny's mother couldn't waste it on what ifs—her mother had told her once that high temperatures can be lowered by bathing the boy in ice cold water and alcohol. Home remedies passed from one generation to another, but she didn't want to deplete her chances. Where could she find ice this time of the night?

What if... Josefa, indeed, was the only one who could help her.

She wrapped Sonny in several sheets and blankets and towels—anything she could find—and took her delirious son. Fever burned in his glazed green eyes. Heavy lidded, the boy made quick jerky movements, as if convulsing, with his arms and legs. He uttered some kind of non-sense spoken too softly for her to be able to decipher.

Like a bird in flight, that night Gris with her son held tight to her bosom flew out of her house and took Sonny to see Josefa. Guilt strapped around her legs. She couldn't move fast enough. As she walked she felt as if she were walking in knee-high mud. Years before, when she had gotten pregnant with Sonny, she had come to see Josefa about getting an abortion. The last thing she needed then was another child. Kenya wasn't even a year old. Josefa said she couldn't help Gris because she, Josefa, had a change of heart.

Gris came in through Josefa's door and sat down on a *taburete*, a wood and cow hide chair. She started to cry so hard that Josefa had to make her some special *tilo* (Linden flowers tea) to calm her down.

'I don't know why,' Gris said. 'God doesn't like me.'

'Nonsense!' Josefa had said, then cleared her throat. 'If God didn't like you he wouldn't let you get this way so often.'

'Rigo doesn't care what happens to me.'

'In this crazy town, everybody knows what kind of man Rigo is. But you continue to sleep with him. *Ese sinverguenza!*'

'He's *my* man.'

Snot ran out of Gris's nostrils and hung over her upper lip. She'd cried like a child. Too bad Josefa couldn't help her then.

THE BOY, too heavy for Gris to carry, made her struggle uphill. Gris tried her best not to stumble and fall.

It was the kind of mean night even dogs feared. Usually the dogs in the neighborhood barked at every passerby, but tonight they hid in their dog houses. She hated those dogs because their owner let them loose and they barked at her whenever she went to the bodega to buy food. Those damned yap-yaps!

She rushed by in silence, and silence was all she heard except for the sound of the rain falling everywhere. The drops of rain fell hard against her skull and shoulders and arms as she hurried up the darkened street. That son of a bitch, she cursed at Rigo. One day she was going to kill that bastard. Cut his balls off, she thought, and feed them to the dogs. From one mean son of a bitch to another.

The road to Josefa's house was muddy. Barefoot, Gris took her chances and tried hard not to trip. Her heels sank into the mud and twice she lost her balance and fell, knees first, against the pebbly surface of the path. Nothing would stop her—not even the rain—from reaching Josefa's house.

Lightning flashed.

Josefa's place wasn't really a house but a shack built awkwardly on termite-ridden stilts. Slanted, it stood to one side of the hill behind the city's dumping grounds. The closer Gris came to the place, the more the sour smell of rotting things choked her. With the end of the blanket she'd wrapped Sonny in she covered her nose and mouth and tried not to breath in that awful stink. She covered her son's face.

Gris reached the porch steps completely out of breath. The floorboards of the porch creaked under her weight. She feared they'd crack open and swallow her into the rat and vermin infested cellar of Josefa's shack. On the door she knocked so hard she scraped her knuckles.

Josefa opened the door. She was holding a candle close to her face. The yellow reflection of the flame illumined her black face and made her eyes look like moons. Cataracts blinded Josefa.

'Oh, *mi santa* Josefa,' Gris said. '*Ayúdame, mujer.* Sonny's very sick.'

'Calm down, *niña,*' Josefa said, opening the door wider to let the mother and child in. *See,* Josefa thought, *it wasn't a cat scratching on the door to be let in. Faculties intact, faculties intact…she was old but not that old. Changó be her guide.*

'I'm sorry to bother you this late—'

'Come,' she said. 'Bring the child to the back room.'

Sonny's mother followed the glow of the candle to a back room that smelled faintly of jasmine.

Though Josefa was short and skinny, her shadow, thrown against the walls by the candle's flickering flame, looked tall and elongated. She walked slowly, her free hand stuck deep in the pocket of the robe she wore. Her feet made a scratching sound on the floor as she walked. Nobody knew how old Josefa was; rumor had it she was over a hundred years old.

In the dark, the walls took on a completely different appearance. They appeared not to be there at all. Gris looked for stars because she swore the walls themselves were the night sky. The night sky like the night skies of her childhood. Clear, deep dark, the stars pockmarked in their corners.

Josefa lit more candles as she told Gris to place the boy on the floor in the middle of the room.

'Remove all the sheets and blankets,' Josefa spoke with compassion. 'Bring the boy out into the open. Gently. Let him breathe.'

Gris did what Josefa said. She placed little Sonny on the wood floor. So that he could be more comfortable, she bundled up one of the blankets into a pillow and placed it under his head. Sonny's eyes were closed; sweat covered his delicate face and forehead.

'He's burning up,' his mother said.

'Remove his clothes too.'

Gris told Josefa about the boy's swollen testicles. 'I'm afraid, Josefa. If I lose—'

'Hush now.'

Clothes off, Sonny lay still on the floor. Gris caressed his face as if rubbing would bring the temperature down. She was no longer paying attention to Josefa, but praying for her boy. The Lord have mercy on her baby—he'd always been such a delicate boy.

Josefa opened a cabinet behind her and rummaged through drawers. She was looking for the right herbs and plants from which to make the potion she would rub over the boy's stomach. His being was being depleted, a mantilla like darkness had fallen over it, was pressing it. Something cold, too, had taken over his warmth. Sonny's belly was swollen and taut like the skin of a drum. She could only guess from the outward position of the boy's bellybutton what the problem was. The boy must have touched the aura of an animal killed by a *santero* for sacrificial purposes, killed with bad intentions.

As Josefa took leaves and powders, mashed and mixed them with her fingers in a small gourd, and added several drops of melted goat's fat, she asked Gris if the boy had behaved differently at some point in the day.

'He plays for hours in the backyard,' she said. 'I don't know. I've been having troubles with my husband. Sonny hears us and thinks his father is going to leave us for good.'

Josefa stood over the boy wiping her hands on a towel she kept on a hook by the side of the cabinet. The ointment was ready. She explained to Gris about Sonny coming in contact with a dead animal that had been sacrificed with ill intentions, used to cause harm.

'Tell me he's not going to die.'

Josefa didn't answer. The boy would not die, but he would never be the same. From the minute she rubbed the ointment over the center of his being, the boy would change. His spirit would no longer be the same, but summoned from a distant place, from another source. But Josefa, having been a mother herself, didn't want to disillusion the mother of the child. She carried the gourd, knelt, and placed it at the child's feet.

Josefa found blood on the boy's skin, rubbed it off with her fingertips, and showed it to Gris. 'This is not the boy's blood,' Josefa said, then noticed that Gris's knees were bleeding. Josefa gave her a towel to wipe the blood. The ointment, she knew from what she had learned long ago from her mother and grandmother, must not be contaminated. It had to be pure.

The *curandera's* dark hands were wrinkled, her skin rough, sandy, worn with use. She started to rub the oily substance outward from the boys belly button. Once she reached the boy's temples, she stopped rubbing, spread his arms and legs out, and rested her hands over his heart. She put her ear to his chest. The boy had a strong heart, she thought, for its beating sounded like the gallop of spooked horses. Josefa put her mouth on the belly button and blew into it as if she were inflating a paper bag. Sonny squirmed then. His hands and feet jerked.

Gris saw the tremor of the boy's eyes behind his eyelids.

'Hold him down,' Josefa told his mother.

It was then that the mother felt the temperature decline. His skin broke out into a sweat. He opened his eyes and looked around, not scared or startled, but as if he'd lived in the room since birth.

Josefa moved away from Gris and the child, back to the cabinet where she wiped the oil off her hands, opened the middle drawer in the cabinet, and removed a bottle of lotion. She uncapped the bottle and poured lotion over her hands. Then she began to shake her hands, sprinkling the lotion all over her body.

Despojo, Changó, *a cleansing of the spirit.* Josefa stood still with her eyes closed, her hands clenched.

Sonny's spirit was purified, no longer taken over by the aura of the dead animal.

'Take him home and let him sleep,' Josefa said. 'In the morning mix a pinch of this with water.'

Gris accepted a small envelope from Josefa. In the bag, Josefa told her, was a special kind of herb that would help protect the child from further harm.

'What do I owe you?' Gris asked.

'*Diez pesos,*' said Josefa.

Sonny's mother asked for Josefa's forgiveness for she didn't have that much money with her. Josefa told her not to worry, that Gris could bring her the money when she had it.

'The boy is no longer lost,' Josefa said.

'How was he lost?'

'No aim. No direction. In his weakness he became susceptible to bad spirits.'

Gris and Sonny spent the night in another bedroom in Josefa's house. The storm passed in the early morning hours. The sun broke through the clouds. Gris awoke to the crowing of a rooster. Next to her, Sonny was sound asleep. She picked up the boy and walked out of the room. Josefa was nowhere in the house, so Gris left.

How she would ever repay the *curandera* Gris didn't know, but Josefa had saved the life of her son.

Southernmost Point

SONNY MANTECA refuses to let go, shake loose. His spirit won't leave my body. Cool Sonny. Crazy Manteca. The best *timbales* player in the world. Sonny full of pizzazz, zest, tropical gusto. Rhythm is Manteca; Manteca is soul, *alma,* bravura, salsa, the mambo, the cha-cha. Sabor Sonny. Sonny, *el cojonudo,* the king of the Latin beat, the drinker, the lady's man, the life-lover, Manteca. The greatest percussionist, a wizard. Manteca, though not an uncommon last name, means lard or grease. I can't stand it anymore, for he's ruining my life, the bastard. Yes, Sonny Manteca is in me. I think you'll know what I mean by the end of this story.

THE TROUBLES with Sonny started when, out of boredom and on Wilfredo's suggestion—a friend at the realty where I worked—that I visit a *santera* or *bruja* or palm reader, I wanted to learn how to play the timbales. I am not a superstitions person, and all that voodoo stuff about *brujeria* or witchcraft has always been beyond me.

The *timbales* are a crucial instrument in any Latin jazz band. They are the two stainless steel drums on a stand, usually with a cowbell between them. To play them has been a childhood dream, that is until the dream became a reality and now a nightmare I can't seem to wake up from.

Before I tell Sonny's story, I will tell mine, but mine is simple. I am second generation Cuban, twenty-eight years old, married to an American woman whose name I won't reveal to spare her or the family any embarrassment, have two lovely children (a boy of seven and a girl of five), and worked at an up-and-coming realty.

Up to now I have been a good husband, father, and a hard worker. Young Cuban-Americans like me are called YUCAS, which stands for Young, Urban, Cuban-American. I'll admit that in my blind search for the American dream I have given up all that is Cuban about me. My parents would readily agree.

I imagine my mother saying: 'His children can't speak Spanish.'

'His children,' says my father, sarcasm forever present in his voice. 'He's forgotten how to speak it himself.'

The old man never liked the idea of me marrying an American woman. He said American women are too cold and indifferent, which isn't true. It's like saying that the Cubans of my generation don't know their mouths from their assholes. That's the thing about Cuban parents and their old values and double standards, they expect the son in the family to marry a member of his own people.

I fell in love with my wife in high school and have been in love with her ever since. She's far from being cold and indifferent. As a matter of fact, she's the one who, after I stopped talking to my father because of an argument, suggested I visit my parents and make up with my father.

My parents claim I've lost all sense of culture. Maybe I have. Just because I don't speak Spanish at home to my children and I don't eat fried plantains, rice and black beans, and pork everyday doesn't mean I'm a lost soul, a terrible person. My heritage is important, sure, but so is my family.

Once in a while I get together with the folks and treat them to Cuban food at a restaurant of their choice. We sit and eat in silence, then whenever my parents speak, I translate for my wife and children. I understand Spanish better than I can speak it, though I practice enough with my Hispanic customers, people, too, whose children will be born and raised Americans.

Anyway, my Americanized way of life is full steam ahead and prospering when one day I get the idea to learn how to play the timbales. Perhaps I dreamt that I could play those damn drums. An idea is an idea, no more and no less, but I fell in deeply for this one.

I thought, Wouldn't it be nice to surprise myself by learning how to do something new, take up a new hobby on the weekends? Maybe if I learned to play well enough I could join a band and show my parents how Cuban I really am.

Nobody knew of this idea, not even my wife, except for Wilfredo, my friend at work whom over lunch one day I told my crazy idea. He looked up from his sandwich and smiled. I thought I knew what he was thinking: this guy has been selling houses too long.

'The *timbales,* huh?' Wilfredo said.

'Why not?' I said. 'I figure it shouldn't be that hard to learn to play them.'

Wilfredo just stared. He is my age, hair growing thinner and grayer by the day. Still single and wild. He, according to my parent's standards, is more Cuban than me. More Cuban in his way of dressing in baggy clothes, no tie and with the top three buttons of his shirt open to expose the chest hair and the gold chains with the San Lazaro and Santa Barbara medallions. More Cuban, yes, in his taste for big assed, large breasted women and greasy, high cholesterol foods. *Chicharrones, ropa vieja, media noches,* and ham *croquetas.*

'I dreamt about it,' I continued.

'About what?' He either hadn't shaved in the last couple of days or had started to grow a beard. Thick stubble darkened his already tanned face.

'Playing the timbales.'

'If you did dream it, then you should buy yourself a set and learn how to play. Nothing to it, if you dreamt you could play.'

Later, on the way back to the realty, Wilfredo recommended I go see this *santera* he knew who read his palm many times and had never been wrong. He gave me her name and number.

'Why would I want to see her?' I asked. 'I don't want her to read my hand.'

'Not for your hand,' he said. 'She'll tell you if you have any talent.'

'I just want to learn how to play, not have talent.'

'Oh, but that's where you're wrong. Without talent it'll be a waste of time.'

'I don't agree.'

'Go see her,' he said. 'If anybody can help you, she can.'

And so, after thinking about the idea for a couple of weeks, I went to see the palm reader.

CALEDONIA the fortuneteller had a *botanica* shop on Sunset Boulevard, near the outskirts of downtown Los Angeles. From the outside the shop looked small and crowded, stuck between two larger buildings, one a furniture retail store and the other a hardware store. A flashing neon sign read CALEDONIA KNOWS ALL. I parked the car in front of the place, locked the doors, and I approached the wrought iron screen door. Where the doorbell was located was a hand, fingers together, painted in white and outlined in black.

I pressed the button twice, waited, then a short Mexican woman appeared behind the screen. Her eyes were too big and black for her small, sad-looking face.

'Do you have appointment?' she asked, her voice sounded tired and withdrawn as though she had been up the whole night talking.

'No,' I said. 'I'd like to make one.'

She unlocked the door and let me in. A thick scent of jasmine incense greeted me in the lobby which was full of shelves and on the shelves stood all kinds of Saint and Virgin statuettes. Also black dolls, African deities, rotting fruit on plates, jars and glasses full of pennies. There were beads arranged in looping W's hanging from the shelves.

Inside a glass counter were miniatures of more saints and virgins, dried mango and mamey seeds. Powders. Cigars. Shiny pebbles. Feather amulets. Charmed ribbons and scrolls. On top of the counter sat an old, heavy looking cash register, the kind with the pop-up numbers, an antique.

'I'm Fabiola,' the woman said. 'Caledonia's spiritual aide.'

I introduced myself and was about to ask for an appointment when a deep, resonant, scratchy voice came from the back room.

'Luis,' the voice said. 'Señor Cuevas?'

'That's me,' I said.

'Wilfredo called in advance.'

I stood there wondering what she meant by in advance.

'Fabiola,' the voice said, 'take the gentleman to consultation room two.'

'*Sí, mi Santa, como no,*' said Fabiola in a Spanish spoken too fast.

Fabiola led me to an even smaller room with nothing but a wicker chair and several pillows strewn on the floor. On the wall in front of me were a row of lit candles. Sunlight snuck in through the blinds. Moats and dust danced in the rays of light.

'Sit down,' Fabiola said. '*La Santisima* will be with you shortly.' Then she closed the door behind her and left me alone in the room. My hands started to sweat as I kept asking myself what I was doing there.

I waited for what felt like a long time. Just when I was about to sit down on the wicker chair, the door opened and a fat woman dressed in a white garb and turban entered the room. She was smoking a cigar whose nasty odor reached my nostrils as quickly as she entered.

Her neck and arms were covered with beads, beads of all colors and sizes. She extended her fat hand for me to shake it, or was it kiss it? She had a pleasant look on her face, baby talcum powder residue clung to her cheeks and chin as if she had just come out of the shower. Her eyes, during that first moment while I shook her hand and gazed into them, seemed to sparkle.

'Luis,' she called my name, then let go of my hand. 'Have a seat.'

'Did Wilfredo tell you why I came to see you?' I asked and sat down on one of the floor pillows.

'He told me about your dream,' she said and sat down on the wicker chair, which cracked and squeaked as she sat. 'I believe I can help you.'

'I'm a bit skeptical.'

'You must tell me about yourself first.'

So. I told her everything I could. About my aspirations to make a lot of money at real estate. Buying and selling fixer-uppers were in my immediate plans. One day I would be able get my broker's license and open my own realty.

'Tell me the truth,' she interrupted. 'Why do you really want to learn how to play the timbales?'

'It's a Cuban thing to do.'

'But you're not Cuban. That is, you don't *feel* Cuban.'

I nodded.

She studied me for a while as if in a trance, then she stood up and called Fabiola. Fabiola opened the door and stuck her head in.

'*Prepara las cosas para una limpieza y llamada,*' Caledonia said, meaning for Fabiola to prepare things for a cleansing and a summons. Then to me, 'Take off your clothes and lie on the floor with your limbs spread out.'

Thinking about Caledonia being nothing but a quack and a fake who was only after cheap thrills, I did what she said to do. While I stripped, she walked around me and poked her finger into places on my back, shoulder blades, stomach, rib cage, thighs, and buttocks. On my belly button, she placed her fist and hit twice, then brought her fist up to her face, closed her eyes and tilted her head back.

Fabiola entered with a tray and placed it on the floor next to the wicker chair. On the tray was a mother-of-pearl handle razor blade, a red and a black pill boxes with some kind of powder or glitter in them. Then Fabiola left the room and returned with a live white dove.

I was stretched out on the floor. Caledonia, barefooted, kept circling above me. On one of her ankles was a tattoo, a symbol I had never seen, and on the other there was an anklet made out of red, white, and black tamarind seeds. She stopped to light her cigar stub, which she turned and turned and chewed in her mouth.

The smoke from the cigar clung to her face and turban and brought her face a distant look of anguish. Fabiola approached Caledonia with her eyes closed, in her hands the dove looked scared. Its head moved nervously.

'Maybe I can come back some other time,' I spoke, but my words no longer affected Caledonia nor Fabiola.

They were both in a trance. Caledonia began to chant in an Afro-Cuban dialect. All I understood were the names, Changó, Elegua, Yemaya—names of African deities.

From the tray Caledonia lifted the razor blade, opened it, then with a swift movement she sliced the head off the dove. The head landed between my legs. Caledonia held the body over me and sprinkled the blood on my chest and stomach.

She was moving so quickly now that I thought she was floating about the room. She was screaming, then she swooped down on me and smeared more blood on my face. Her cold hands rubbed my arms and legs.

By now I had my eyes closed. I didn't want to see the mess. It was then I got the shivers. Convulsions came and went and I lost all sense of time and space. I must have fallen asleep because when I awoke, I was clean and a towel covered my naked mid section. I was still on the floor, a pillow under my head. Caledonia and Fabiola were gone.

I stood up and got dressed, feeling angry and disappointed. I thought I had been made a fool of.

Fabiola was behind the counter and cash register in the front room. She acted as though nothing had happened. I told her I wanted to see Caledonia.

'Oh, Mr Cuevas,' she said. 'Come back tomorrow. She is asleep now. She told me to tell you that the spirit is in you.'

'Spirit?'

'The person she summoned to help you.'

Fabiola wrote down on a receipt the amount I owed her and the time I was to return the next day. I paid her and left the place more confused than angry, with an incredible thirst and hunger. *The person she summoned to help you,* the words followed me home.

'SONNY WHO?' I asked Caledonia the next day. We were sitting in another room, this one larger and with more comfortable furniture.

'Manteca,' she said. 'His name is Sonny Manteca. He will be your guide.'

She proceeded to tell me his story:

Sonny Manteca was a *mulato* from Kalimete, a small town in the province of Las Villas, Cuba. He was born there in 1929, and two years later when the depression hit the island, his family, which was poor already, had no other alternative than to pack up and move to Havana. His brothers and sisters, seven in total, were all much older than Sonny.

His father, once in the big city, abandoned the family and left Sonny's mother to struggle for survival. They lived in a small, dirt floor shack on the fringes of the city. Everyday Sonny went with his mother to the market or to the Almendares River to wash clothes. She did laundry for other families for ten cents a load. Sonny loved his mother and he grew up hating what she had to do feed the family.

All of Sonny's brothers and sisters left the house by the time they reached fifteen years of age and made their way into the world. Sonny, being the youngest, refused to leave his mother.

In the city he found work as a dishwasher in a small night club. Most days he worked from six in the morning until nine or ten o'clock at night when the club's band was arriving and setting up. Once in a while he would stay to listen to the music, but by then he was exhausted and would fall asleep in the back of the kitchen on top of a long wooden bench.

On break the musicians would come to the kitchen and eat and drink. It was there that Sonny befriended the conga player, a black man who was balding but had a crown of graying hair from ear to ear. His name was Guiro. Guiro taught Sonny to play the *tumbadoras* and congas. Sonny learned so quickly and was so good that Guiro would let him sit in on some of the last sets of the night.

Then Guiro died and Sonny took his place and began to make a little money. Whatever little money Sonny made he gave to his mother, so, he said, she wouldn't have to wash dirty laundry.

The years passed and Sonny learned to master not only the congas and *tumbas,* but the timbales as well. He liked the timbales better than any of the other instruments. Its sound was crisper, sharper, more resonant. He also liked playing center stage which is where the timbales player sets up. With Sonny playing the timbales the band got to be known in the right circles in Havana. More people came for the late shows. The restaurant owner, one night, gave everyone a raise.

Sonny's mother, who was becoming suspicious as to how Sonny was getting so much money, decided to come to the club one night and she cried when she saw her son playing so beautifully. She was so happy that she started to dance to the rhythm of her son's beat.

In 1956 a talent scout found Sonny at the club and offered him a position to play with the inventor and king of the mambo, Perez Prado. Sonny Manteca was riding high now. On top, there was no way for him to come down. He bought his mother a house, then taught her how to drive and bought her a car. The Perez Prado orchestra toured the continent. They played all over Europe. Sonny loved Paris, Madrid, and London.

Upon their return to Cuba, Sonny met and fell in love with a beautiful white woman. She had black hair and blue eyes and when she danced she made other couples stop dancing and look at her. Their affair was a secret one, meeting at a beach house in Varadero.

One year before the triumph of the revolution, Perez Prado left the band and flew to Mexico where he owned a house. After so many years, the band found itself without its leader. Sonny himself was contemplating eloping with his white goddess, but her jealous brother found out about their affair and one night, during the taping of a television show, waited outside the studios for Sonny and his sister to come out.

It was one of those gorgeous tropical nights when the heat and humidity were swept away by a sea breeze. The light of the moon shone off the cars parked up and down the street. The whole city seemed to be enjoying the evening for there was music and laughter coming out of tenement windows. Couples walked out of cafes and movie houses embracing, kissing, wondering what the night was really made for.

The stalker waited and waited until finally Sonny walked out of the studio entrance. He had his arm around his white woman. Before he reached the car, the woman's brother came out of his hiding place, shot Sonny, and ran.

Sonny Manteca died with a bullet in his heart.

THAT SAME NIGHT after Caledonia told me Sonny's story I couldn't sleep. Something in me was set astir. I sat up against the propped pillows on the headrest and thought about my comfortable life, my wife sound asleep next to me, my two children in the room next door. Comfortable, I thought, and in the end what does it all mean?

There were dogs howling very far away.

Sarah rolled over in her sleep. Her face looked calm, her parted blondish hair exposing her wide forehead. The sheet slid off her chest and one of her breasts came out into the open. Her wrinkled nipple stood erect. From the cold, I thought, unless she's dreaming about....

Then Sonny Manteca took over me for the first time. I felt him do it. Without speaking he made me slide down the mattress to where Sarah's ass would be under the sheet. I pulled the sheet up and started to kiss her behind, got my head between her legs. She woke up then with a moan, held my head there and writhed. Sonny's passion had been bottled up too long. Somebody popped the cork and let them out. Sarah couldn't believe me.

I wouldn't stop making love to her until she had three orgasms, the last one shook her hard. She screamed.

'For god's sakes,' I said. 'You'll wake up the children.'

'Never mind the children,' she said. 'What has come over you?'

Sonny Manteca, I wanted to say. The bastard. The conniving, son of a bitch, who rendered me helpless while he made love to my wife. *You asked for it,* I felt him say.

By morning I wasn't myself any more. As I sat at the breakfast table, Sonny greeted my wife with a long kiss on the lips, then my children with surprise. Of course, he'd never had any of his own. He liked them though, and they immediately grew fond of him.

When the school bus came and took the children, Sarah came to the bedroom where I was dressing and asked to be made love to again. There went Sonny, the pleaser.

'Oh, Luis,' she said. 'I feel something wonderful happening here.'

'So do I,' I said, but it was Sonny doing the talking.

'Honey,' she said when we were through. 'Don't forget to get Lindy a birthday gift.'

Would I forget to get my own daughter a gift? 'I've got plenty of time,' I said. 'Her birthday isn't until this weekend.'

But I never made it.

As soon as I got to the office, I called Caledonia and heard the message on her answering machine: It said they would be gone on vacation for two weeks. Two weeks, fucking rotten luck. Wilfredo walked by and I shouted at him to get his ass in my office.

'You and your fucking bright ideas,' I told him.

'What's the problem, brother?' he said in this isn't-it-nice-to-be-alive-this-morning tone of voice that rubbed me the wrong way.

I told him what had happened and all he could do was laugh. He took a cigarette out of his shirt pocket and lit it.

'I have this urge now,' I told him. 'To buy the finest set of timbales, lock myself up in a garage and practice. Practice and do a little drinking.'

'I know this music store,' he said and exhaled.

'Don't help him, help me!' I stood up and straightened out my shirt. 'Let's not waste time, take me there.'

We drove on the freeway and got to the music store ten minutes before it opened. There was a cafeteria at the corner so we went and had a cup of coffee, which Sonny didn't like. It was too watery. He was used to drinking the Cuban espresso, strong and sweet.

'Who said I'm not Cuban enough?' I asked.

'Nobody said it,' Wilfredo said. 'You were the one who felt not submerged in the culture.'

'How do you feel?'

'As Cuban as I am American?'

'That doesn't tell me shit.'

'It's not supposed to,' he said and drank his murky creamed coffee. 'We've spent more time in this country than in the other.'

'Do you ever wish you could go back?'

'Not really. What would I go back for? My family's here.'

'A way of life.'

'A way of life is a way of life. We live here, we fuck here, we have fun here, we die here—that's a way of life too.'

We left the café and returned to the music store. It was open. The minute I stepped inside Sonny Manteca went wild. It was as if a child had walked into a toy store. He took me to the percussion section where he found what he was looking for: the best set of timbales.

He shouted at one of the salesmen to bring him a set of sticks. Luckily there were no other customers except for Wilfredo and myself, and Wilfredo wasn't buying.

The salesman, a chubby man in his early forties, brought the sticks over and with a tinge of reluctance handed them to me. The round tipped sticks felt awkward in my hands, but not for Sonny.

He played as if he were playing in front of a large audience. Both Wilfredo and the salesman stared with bewildered smiles on their faces. They couldn't believe the sound; I couldn't believe it myself. Boy, could Sonny bang on those drums. He kept a steady, exuberant beat. The drumming went: Truc! Truc! Trac-tac, tricky-ticky, trac-tac! Tuc! Tuc!

Some of the people inside a cubicle office came out to listen.

'Who's the guy?' the salesman asked Wilfredo.

'A real estate agent.'

The salesman looked at Wilfredo in disbelief.

'I want these,' Sonny Manteca shouted.

'Those are the best we've got,' said the salesman.

'We'll take them,' Wilfredo said.

Sonny Manteca's blood rushed through me. His was an uncontrollable ecstasy. In his happiness I found mine. It was the sudden realization that something as easy as playing the drums could make me feel that good. Giddy with pleasure, I paid for the drums and took them to Wilfredo's garage where I played and played, played and didn't return to work, played and didn't stop to eat the food Wilfredo ordered, played until the next door neighbors called the cops and they came and told us to stop making so much racket, played after they left, and finally played until Sarah called to find out when I was going home. Wilfredo, sleepy and tired and with a splitting headache he said would never stop until I stopped playing, dragged me out of the garage and closed the door. It was then and only then that Sonny Manteca let me go home.

THE NEXT COUPLE of days I called around other *botanicas* but nobody I spoke to said they could help my situation. One man told me that once a spirit was summoned, the only person who could make it go away was the person who summoned it. Tough luck, no. I phoned Caledonia, but the machine answered. I felt like leaving the following message: Caledonia, you whore, where the fuck are you?

Sonny wanted to find a band to play with.

At Miami Spice, a small artsy-fartsy, art deco imitation restaurant nightclub, there was a Latin jazz band playing salsa. I was at the bar having a Black Russian when Sonny Manteca decided to approach the conga player and asked if he could play the timbales.

The conga player was a bit hesitant at first, but when I stood behind the timbales and began to play he smiled an all white teeth smile. It was as if he recognized the beat. When it was time for a solo, Sonny jumped in and performed awesomely. He thrilled the audience with his drumming antics. The timbales sang out in jubilant rhythm.

When it was over all the band members wanted to talk to me. The leader was talking about my joining the band. I told them I'd think about it. Sonny needed a drink so I went to the bar and ordered another drink.

'That was great,' said the bartender. 'This one's on the house.'

A tall black woman approached me and told me how she'd never seen anybody play with so much energy. She felt the rhythm all over her body. Her hands went up on the inside of my thighs to my crotch.

'I felt it right there,' she said and squeezed.

Sonny Manteca wasted no time. He led me and the woman outside to the parking lot and behind in the alley way, he lowered her panties and straddled her from behind. The alcohol rushed to my head and I lost control. I made love to that black woman like never before to any other woman, like Sonny Manteca played the timbales: hard, relentlessly keeping the beat.

After we were done we returned inside to the bar and I ordered another round. The black woman drank and rubbed the cold glass over her sweating forehead. She licked at the ice cubes.

Shivers started to run up and down my spine. I felt strange, as though Sonny Manteca was leaving. I finished that drink and ordered another. The more I drank the better I felt.

'Hey, brother, have you ever felt the blues?' Sonny said.

'We better go home,' I said. 'I have to shop for a birthday gift tomorrow.'

On impulse, I kissed the black woman and told her I had to go. She looked satisfied enough not to complain, besides I told her I might see her around again.

In the car on the way home, Sonny again asked if I had ever felt the blues.

'In real estate you have no time to feel anything,' I told him.

'I want to go back home,' he said. 'This is gringoland here, man, and I don't feel good. Back home is where the action is. The clubs, the people, the greatest musicians in the world.'

Sonny Manteca told me about how great living in the island was. Those endless hot summers and the girls at the beach. The carnivals in Havana, the *comparsas* and the floats and the women dancers with their glittering costumes...Sonny grew quiet, withdrew to his own thoughts.

I made it home all right and parked the car in the driveway. Inside I tiptoed to the bedroom, took off my clothes, and snuck into bed next to Sarah. I fell asleep quickly and dreamt of ways I'd never be.

THE FOLLOWING AFTERNOON I went shopping for a birthday gift for my four year old baby girl and he took control. I was going by the shoe department at the Buffums in Cerritos shopping center when I suddenly stopped and Sonny Manteca decided to have me try on a pair of boots.

'Man, look at those boots. Leather and suede, slanted heels, brass tips. I want them,' he said in his casual drunken, soft-spoken voice. 'Buy them or I'll grab a salesgirl's ass.'

'Which one?' I said, looking around for the nearest salesgirl on the chance that I might warn her in time.

'Try them on. Get them in brown.'

All around me were shoes and more shoes and nothing but shoes. Not knowing what Sonny would want me to do next, I took the brown boot on the display and held it. It was suede all right; it felt smooth even though the leather was cracked and scratched to give it a worn look. The price tag read $150.

'Sonny, I don't have this much cash on me,' I said.

'Haven't you ever heard of plastic, baby?' he said. 'Use your bank card.'

'How do you know I have credit cards?'

'*Coño, compai,* what do you take me for? A fool. What's yours is mine, no?'

'Look, I'm not—'

'What are you waiting for?' His thick Cuban accent was getting the best of me. 'Here comes the salesgirl.'

A salesgirl, tall and slender with too much make up on her face, approached me and asked what she could help me with. Needless to say I was tongue tied, but not Sonny—he's never at a loss for words.

'Hey, sugar,' he said. I blushed, showing her the boots. 'How about a pair of these in size nine.'

The salesgirl flashed a nervous smile, a you've-got-to-be-kidding look appeared on her pale face.

'Come on, Blancanieves,' he said, meaning Snow White. He took control of my hands. I feared what he might do so I dug them deep in my pockets and closed my fingers tight around the lining.

'Move it, sweets. Size nine, okay?' Sonny told her.

The salesgirl walked away into the stockroom through the curtains behind the cash register. I sat down in the nearest chair, feeling wired, nerves on edge. From what I knew so far about Sonny, I knew he could push me over.

'Wassimatter, Cubichon?' he said. 'You gotta relax, amigo. Take it easy for a change. The problem with you is you're too used to the gringo life.'

The salesgirl returned with three boxes and placed them on the chair next to me. 'You know what?' she said, removing the cardboard lid from the box on top. 'I don't have a nine in the brown. I have it in black. I brought an eight and a half and a nine and a half in brown. Try it on.'

I removed my right shoe and quickly tried on all the boots. The eight and a half fit too tight and the nine and a half too loose. The black in a nine fit perfect.

'I'll take these,' I said to the salesgirl who stood at a distance in front of me.

'Cash or charge?'

'Visa,' I said and took the other boot from the box. 'I think I'll take them on.'

'Sure,' she said and walked to the register where she ran the card through the scanner for an authorization number, then, while she waited, she rang up the sale and printed a sales ticket and had it ready for me to sign.

'Go to men's wear,' said Sonny, and before I could stop my legs I was on my way there.

'Hey, wait,' the salesgirl said after me.

'Keep it cool, darling,' he said. 'I'll be right back.'

In the men's department he had me browse until he stumbled upon a pair of flower print bermudas. 'Try these on,' he said.

'Screw you,' I said. 'I'm leaving.'

'Come on, *asere,* don't make me force you. Be a nice guy. Besides I didn't ask for you, remember? You asked for me.'

He took me to one of the dressing room stalls and made me try the bermudas on. There I stood in front of the mirror, dressed in the funny looking shorts and the pair of black boots. What a ridiculous sight!

There was a knock on the door. It was the shoe department salesgirl with my card and the receipt slip for me to sign. Persistent little bitch, I thought.

'You're—how do you say—' began Sonny. 'A persistent little bitch.'

The salesgirl threw the piece of paper and a pen at me. 'Asshole,' she said. 'I'm calling security—' and she was gone.

'Shit,' I said.

'I think we better scram, you know, before the manager comes.'

'Manager,' I said, putting my pants back on, forgetting I was leaving the bermudas on underneath. 'Didn't you hear her? She said she was calling security. The cops.'

'So move it, slow poke.'

Too late. By the time I made it out of the stall, the salesgirl was back with a tall, robust, black security guard. Caught red handed, so they

say. The salesgirl had this malicious smile on her lips. She was probably saying to herself, I'm glad you got caught you little pervert. I was
angry. Sonny was feeling rather pissed. The security guard had the
cuffs ready and when he tried to get them on me, I knocked the lights
out of him, or, rather Sonny did it. The guard fell like a huge tree falls
in the forest: quickly and heavily.

The salesgirl screamed.

Sonny made me run away, part of the bermuda's sticking out of my
opened fly. It was hard to run in the new boots. By the time I made it
outside and found my car, I was sweating profusely. The high noon sun
felt like a torch against my skin. I opened the door of the car, jumped in
and saw on the rear view mirror more security guards coming. Who'd
believe the story about Sonny's spirit taking over my body?

I started the car and stepped on the gas as hard as I could. The car
flew out of the parking spot.

'You forgot the plastic, man,' Sonny said.

'To hell with you and the plastic,' I said. There was so much fury in
me that I felt like banging my head on the dashboard until Sonny came
out, but instead I drove like a lunatic to the freeway on-ramp and took
the fast lane north.

MR MANTECA tells me we're headed in the right direction as we
continue down the road. He's feeling the blues. I'm feeling them too,
longing to be home with my wife and kids. Key West is the right direction, our destination. I don't know why, but I don't ask. He's taken over,
so I drive. Am I crazy? Maybe, but I doubt it. All that matters is that the
spirit of Sonny Manteca is in me and won't let go. He's got his reasons;
I have mine.

Driving cross country is his idea, not mine. The driving, though, is
relaxing, almost comforting. It provides enough peace and tranquili-
ty for recollection. Clarity of thought. Let me, if I may, begin from the
end and work my way to the beginning. By now I'm probably wanted
in the State of California for shoplifting and God knows what else—
only Sonny knows the truth, only he can tell me.